Love is
a time of enchantment:
in it all days are fair and all fields
green. Youth is blest by it,
old age made benign:
the eyes of love see
roses blooming in December,
and sunshine through rain. Verily
is the time of true-love
a time of enchantment — and
Oh! how eager is woman
to be bewitched!

THE FRENCH COUNTESS

In the year 1789 Magdalena, a young French Countess, was surrounded by luxury and her future seemed assured. At the same time, in an Essex village, George Mitchell was wrestling with the problem of providing for his widowed mother and his brothers and sisters. The Revolution in France and declaration of war between France and England were to cause a dramatic upheaval in the lives of the Countess and the humble English yeoman. Each was faced by apparently insuperable difficulties until fate brought them together.

Books by Betty King
in the Ulverscroft Large Print Series:

WE ARE TOMORROW'S PAST

BETTY KING

THE FRENCH COUNTESS

Complete and Unabridged

ULVERSCROFT
Leicester

First published in Great Britain in 1982 by
Robert Hale Limited
London

First Large Print Edition
published September 1994
by arrangement with
Robert Hale Limited
London

British Library CIP Data

King, Betty
 The French countess.—Large print ed.—
Ulverscroft large print series: romance
I. Title
823.914 [F]

ISBN 0–7089–3148–0

Published by
F. A. Thorpe (Publishing) Ltd.
Anstey, Leicestershire
Set by Words & Graphics Ltd.
Anstey, Leicestershire
Printed and bound in Great Britain by
T. J. Press (Padstow) Ltd., Padstow, Cornwall

This book is printed on acid-free paper

To the gentle memory of
my grandmother,
Alice Maria Magdalene Gates,
1870 – 1963,
born in Cape Province

If love were what the rose is,
And I were like the leaf,
Our lives would grow together
In sad or singing weather,
Blown fields or flowerful closes
Green pleasures or grey grief.

Algernon Charles Swinburne
1837 – 1909

Acknowledgements

My especial gratitude is due to my niece, Felicity Gawthorne, who deciphered my handwriting, typed and edited the script, Arthur Rose, Esq., who supplied several of the nautical details, the staffs of the London Library and the White Hart Hotel, Salisbury, who looked after me for a time, Joan Sharp and Wendi Claxton.

Bibliography

England in the Eighteenth Century,
J. H. Plumb. Pelican Books.

*The Companion Guide to the South
of France,* A. Lyall. Collins, 1978.

*The French Noblesse of the Eighteenth
Century.* Marquise de Créquy, 1834.
Trans. Mrs Coloquhoun Grant.
John Murray, 1904.

The Bourbon Tragedy, Rupert Furneaux.
Allen & Unwin, 1968.

Southern France, Muirhead and
Monmarche. Macmillan, 1926.

Baedeker's Southern France, 1899.

Nelson, Carola Oman. Hodder &
Stoughton, 1947.

Nelson and the Hamiltons, Jack
Russell. Anthony Blond, 1969.

Fighting Sail, A. B. C. Whipple and
the Editors of Time-Life Books,
1978.

1

THE village of Helmdon stands on a slight rise of ground above the marshes of eastern Essex. From the square tower of the Norman church, set back from a cluster of small houses, it is possible to see for miles across the barren wastes of grey-green land to the equally uniform flatness of the North Sea. There is nothing but this endless vista of the unknown to distinguish the place from a hundred such others, but to George Mitchell the sea was as alluring as any siren's song of old.

On a November day in 1789 he was guiding the plough-horse through the heavy, clay soil of the twenty-acre field which sloped upwards to the farmhouse where he lived. As he tugged on the slippery reins he wrestled with the ancient plough which had already outlived three generations of his family. His toil did nothing to relieve his rebellious and despondent frame of mind, for it was raining with set-in determination and, despite his leather jacket, he was soaked to the skin. There was nothing particularly new in this experience for one who spent most of his waking hours cultivating the protesting earth, but on this occasion he longed, with a need bordering on passion, to be in the huge, warm kitchen of his home listening with his younger brothers and sisters to his Uncle Samuel. His dead father's kinsman came so rarely to Langetts that it was a sin to waste a moment of his time.

Tall for his seventeen years with a frame that promised to fill out as he matured George's drenched face and gloomy scowl gave only a hint of the good features, dark hair and expressive eyes which made most of the village girls court his attention when they met. George was not averse to this flattery, although he still blushed scarlet whenever his siblings taunted him with his conquests. So far he had been able to keep from them the knowledge that Bess, the daughter of the ale-house keeper, was prepared to favour him further than offering her cheek for kisses at harvest-home suppers. Yet he was already aware that the snatched embraces and over-eager lips were not his idea of what he wanted from a girl: Bess was too anxious to please, too ready to press her comely body against his.

He called out a gruff command to the horse as they reached the summit of the hill, and he caught sight of faint candle-glimmer from the kitchen window. One more downward furrow and one more home and that was his stint for the day.

As he held the well-polished blade in position he imagined the scene around the open hearth. His mother, tall and gaunt, the five girls waiting on Samuel and the two younger boys, who favoured their dead father, listening intently to their uncle. Not for the first time he pondered the unanswerable question of why his mother disliked him so very much. Could it be that she resented the fact that he still lived while his father, for whom she had given up her inheritance, lay beneath the turf of the nearby churchyard? He had discovered, in the books which she had taught him

3

to read, that mothers usually favoured their sons; this was certainly not so in his own case. Although he did everything possible to keep the small farm well enough to pay the rent and provide a meagre diet throughout the year she still found fault with him, calling him boorish, ill-mannered and secretive.

George was willing to admit to the last because he did live in a world of his own, where his bed was not shared by Joseph and Reuben, his twin brothers, nor his every waking hour in the farmhouse filled with the nagging voice of his mother.

George understood, too well, the main reason why his parent was so embittered. Sarah Copping had been the only child of William Copping, lord of the manor of Helmdon, whose house stood less than a quarter of a mile from where he now trudged downwards towards the lane. When she had married beneath her and come, against the wishes of her father and mother, to live at Langetts, she had forfeited her birthright and had never exchanged a further word with her parents. Soon after the marriage his grandparents had sold the manor house to a local brewer with rising fortunes and disappeared no one knew whither. While George's father lived Sarah had been able to withstand the unkindness with which she had been treated and had doted upon the elder George with a dedication verging on idolatry. His son remembered him as a fair giant of a man, surprisingly gentle despite his large bulk, and deeply attached to the woman who had sacrificed her known world for his alien one. Although George saw his father kiss his mother and embrace her on rare occasions of family celebration or relief the passion which must have attracted each to the other was not obviously apparent: only the eight children bearing witness to the secret satisfaction concealed behind the largest room in the house which had been (and still was) his mother's bedroom. The elder George had loved his offspring, but until the dropsy carried him off to an early grave it was Sarah who mattered the most.

In the first shock of her widowhood Sarah had retired to the sloping-roofed bedroom and remained there, without food and drinking only the water which George placed ready for her each day, for a week. At the end of these seven, endless days she reappeared almost unrecognisable as the handsome out-going woman she had so recently been. Her face had sunken, and her high cheek-bones now only accentuated the hollow depth of her eyes. Her shoulders stooped, her bosom sagged, she seemed to have shrunk in stature, and with her good looks had gone her sanguine temperament. Although still meticulous in her dress and her house-keeping she never smiled, and frequently spoke to the five girls as if they were hirelings picked up as leavings at a servants' fair. George was surprised that his sisters did not resent this unfair treatment, but he imagined that they must have more understanding than he, for they still tried, in the face of heavy odds, to please their mother. Only the twins, now seven, seemed able to arouse any warmth in Sarah, and on one occasion, when Joseph had fallen out of an apple tree and landed on his neck, had George surprised a look of loving anguish on their mother's face.

Nearing the hedge George realised that the rain had stopped and the wind veered to the north-east. He smelt the salt tang of the invisible sea beyond the darkling marshes and he stopped to take deep breaths. On just such an evening his father would have suggested that the pair of them rise early the next day and take the punt to seek for water-fowl.

George turned the horse and pushed with renewed vigour towards the farmhouse: perhaps Uncle Samuel would like an outing on the morrow.

★ ★ ★

The family was already eating the day's main meal when George came out of the lean-to in dry clothes. His uncle rose immediately from the table and embraced him in a warm and kindly manner. "My boy, grown to be a man!" Samuel turned to his sister-in-law. "You did not tell me, Sarah."

"What to tell? All children grow to be adults if the Lord doesn't see fit to carry them off — and the way George eats 'tis no wonder he's enormous."

As George sat to take the plate of suet pudding and red, roast mutton which his eldest sister brought to him from the hearth he felt, rather than saw, the look with which Samuel regarded Sarah. For a moment there was silence, and then Joseph begged Samuel to retell the story of how one of his seamen had jumped ship as they were casting off and had landed on the cobbled quay to break his back.

"Not while we're eating," Sarah rebuked him. "Look to your food and hold your tongue."

One of the girls asked shyly if they might hear the story of the marmoset Samuel had bought in a North African port and which he had brought safely as far as the Bay of Biscay in a linen basket only to have the tiny creature turn its face to the bulkhead and die without warning. Samuel told this heart-rending epic with many embroideries and side anecdotes until George's plate was clean and the girls were serving a dish of baked apples and custard.

"You must tend the farm well to feed such a family," Samuel said to George.

George blushed and mumbled his thanks, busy about the task of eating his food so that he should not hear his mother's crushing rejoinder to this unlooked-for praise. One of the girls caused a diversion at this point by dropping the jug of ale she had been sent to bring from the still-room, and George studied his uncle as he watched the mopping-up process.

Samuel Mitchell, younger than George's father by eighteen months or so, must have been forty years of age. Unlike his elder brother his hair was russet brown rather than fair, and although large-framed his body had a lean suppleness which was contrary to all that George had heard of his grandfather and grand-uncles. He had been apprenticed in early youth to a master of a small trading vessel which plied between Colchester and the Netherlands and had done so well that he was now part-owner of a ship of his own. George envied him with an intensity his mother would have called sinful: his favourite daydream consisting of being asked by Samuel to quit Langetts and take up a sea-faring life. But how could he do that? How leave a widow (however unloving and ungrateful) to oversee a farm of some fifty acres while he followed his own most selfish ends? If only the sixteen-year-old Patience had been a boy things might have been different, but it would be years yet before the twins were able to do more than stook corn or turn hay. True enough the girls milked, made butter and saw to the hens, but they could not be expected to assist at calving nor help with sheep dipping and tarring.

George had no money of his own and no possessions, his mother doling out to him a few pence to buy ale while she fashioned his clothes from the homespun woollen cloth she made herself. He was, he found himself thinking as he watched the firelight play on the wind-darkened skin of his uncle's face, little better than an unrespected slave. Even his sisters, taking their cue from their mother, treated him warily, teasing him only when she was absent about some mysterious business of her own. Occasionally Lydia, the youngest, made bold enough to touch him and had been the sole member on his last birthday to remember the day and bring him a kerchief for his midday bread and cheese which she had painstakingly fashioned from one of her own old petticoats.

He was surprised out of his melancholy thoughts by his uncle's voice: "Well then, George, don't you want to come then?" George looked up and saw that the females had departed to the scullery where they were rinsing the dishes in the wooden tub. He and his uncle were alone. "You'll be needing a sup of ale after that day's ploughing, I be thinking."

Gratefully, George smiled and followed Samuel out into the cold night.

★ ★ ★

In the snug of The Plough it was warm and cosy, a large fire burning in the ingle nook. Several men were already seated on the settles at the hearth, and George and Samuel took their pewter tankards of strong ale from the landlord and retired to a corner of the room. George was glad that Bess was not present.

"It was good of you to bring me those

shirts and the pair of nankeen breeches," George said after both men had taken a long pull at their ale. "And the girls were highly pleased with the bolts of silk; it'll give them something to do in the winter making dresses for the spring. I don't expect any of them ever thought to have a garment of such fine quality, and Lydia looked at you as if she believed you to be a fairy godmother."

"A fine godmother *I'd* make!" Samuel chuckled. "But what's a bachelor uncle for if it's not to provide something a little different from day-to-day fare."

"You bring that by just coming to Langetts."

Samuel regarded him for a moment, but murmured something about that being his pleasure and went on to ask his nephew what he thought about the violent upheaval of revolution in France.

"It doesn't seem to make a great deal of difference down here," George shrugged. "The smuggling at West Mersea goes on just the same across the Channel. It's only when I go into Colchester with stock for sale that I hear talk of how men's minds are turning."

"What would you say was the general opinion?"

"It depends largely on the size of the speaker's land — large landowners are utterly against the Jacobins, while labourers and tenants are prepared to accept that the rebels have some sort of right to determine their own way of life."

"Have they not such a right, think you?" Samuel's tone was mild.

"Are you a Whig, Uncle Sam?" George was frankly incredulous.

"I'm no political partisan, but Charles Fox has a case when he maintains that, though the sans-culottes have taken the wrong road, they have a right to seek their own destination."

"But I hear that they commit the most terrible acts upon the nobility — that must surely be wrong."

"Of course, but once power has come into the hands of those unused to its heady influence it's like a man suddenly finding brandy for the first time and draining a bottle at a sitting."

"You don't think that England will ever see such a state of affairs? We've been near enough to it, my father told me, in the past."

"The English are too practical — and lazy — to fly to such lengths, but the politicians would be wise to ease the burdens of the poor and give them a greater share of the wealth which is coming in the wake of industrial growth."

"From what I hear Prinny spends most of that!"

"If all the tales be true — and I grant there are some stories." Samuel proceeded to relate some of the more salacious anecdotes he had heard on his travels, and George felt a glow of gratitude that his uncle considered him old enough to listen to such gossip; it was certainly a change from the treatment he received at home. He thought about this while Samuel went to the counter to replenish their tankards, his smile fading as he remembered his mother's cantankerous and unwarranted behaviour and his face resuming the melancholy expression which his uncle's ribaldry had dispelled.

When they had sat sipping for a few

moments Samuel surprised his nephew by asking him directly: "Are you not happy at home, boy?"

George gulped with his mouth to the rim of the beaker. Taken off guard he answered that he had not thought about the matter in a straightforward way, but that he supposed if the truth was known he was dispirited with his life at Langetts.

"Your mother is a sick woman," Samuel stated flatly.

"She never ails."

"I mean sick in the mind."

"But there is no madness in the family."

"She is by no means a case for the asylum, if that's what you're thinking, but I believe that since my brother died the corner-stone of her life has been knocked away and this has altered her outlook on her very existence."

"You know that, after Father died, she shut herself in their bedroom and starved herself for a week?"

"I'd guessed as much for she was a fine figure of a woman." Samuel regarded George intently. "She did not always

15

single you out for blame as she does now?"

George shook his head. "We were always less to her than my father and she was often shrewish, but I put that down to the fact that she had been bred to a more gentle life than the farm offered and she was not used to the hundreds of distasteful tasks she was called upon to do."

"A shrewd judgement — I see that you've inherited your grandfather's brains."

"Mitchell or Copping?"

"Well, my father was a canny old countryman, but it was the grandiose grandsire I was thinking of: a Cambridge man, no less, and heartbroken to see his daughter wed with a common tenant farmer when he'd set his sights on a son from one of the best county families."

"There's nothing wrong with our family," George protested stoutly, defending the father he missed most sadly. "Do you think it is because Mother realises that she could have done better for herself that she resents us — and me in particular?"

Samuel did not reply immediately, and

then he said, deliberately, "If you ask me, I think your mother is one of those women who love the man of their choice more than their offspring. When she and my brother had to marry — "

"*Had* to marry?" George cried.

"'Twas the only way the matter could be resolved: and as I was saying I think it was George she wanted, and she found the raising of children more than she bargained for. 'Tis a pity ladies can't practise the arts of the whores — that'd soon make for smaller families."

George hardly heard this reflection on society as he wrestled with the knowledge that he had been the direct cause of his parent's marriage. "Do you think they'd not have wed if I'd not been on the way?"

Samuel stared at him. "Not wed?" he laughed. "Nothing could have stopped them — they were the most moonstruck lovers I've ever set eyes on." He patted George's shoulder and went to the landlord to refill the pewter mugs. On his return he said: "Now, don't you go fretting yourself about anything I've told you — I spoke to you mainly to ease your mind." He drank deeply, wiping his mouth with the back of his hand. "I suppose you've never thought of going to sea?"

George was startled out of his melancholy thoughts. "When I've time to think of anything else but seed-corn, mulching, muck-spreading and reaping I dream of leaving it all and following you."

"Then why don't you do it, boy?"

"It's impossible. Who'd look after Langetts until the twins are older?"

"A hired man."

"We've no money." George's tone was flat.

"I'm not rich but I've put away a tidy sum which'll come to you, and I figure you might as well benefit from it now as later."

Samuel's wealth had been a topic much discussed between Sarah and her husband in the old days, and its import had not been lost on the long ears of the children. "But you might marry," George said, unconsciously voicing the opinions he had overheard.

"I'll not wed now. The girl I loved couldn't wait for me and married a baker from Rowhedge — none too happy, either, so I hear — but that's neither here nor there for it's not much life for the wife of a sailor come to think of it: months of being alone."

There was silence for a moment or two, the only sounds in the room being the click of dominoes on a polished table and a log rolling from the andirons onto the hearth.

"Would you really do that for me, Uncle Sam?"

"Willingly, lad. It's not all a one-sided affair — I could do with an apprentice mate."

"How shall I set about the business?"

"Leave it to me. I know the bailiff at the manor; many's the pheasant we brought home together when we were young."

"Weren't you afraid of being deported?"

"Nowhere to go to after America was lost to us — until they discovered Botany Bay."

"I can't see how the gentry think they own the birds of the air."

"Neither could I, and that's why I took them," Samuel chuckled. "Well, now that we've settled that matter tell me the village gossip not fit for the females' ears."

At this juncture two of Samuel's old cronies came in, bringing a blast of raw air, and Bess appeared from the kitchen. George talked with her in a desultory fashion, but he was too full of his uncle's suggestion to give her much attention, and after a while she left him with a distinct air of pique.

On the way home George asked his uncle what he should do about telling his mother his future plans. "Say nothing, lad, until we find the right fellow to take your place; then you can face her with an accomplished fact rather than a hope."

★ ★ ★

In the event Samuel was over-optimistic in his hopes of finding a replacement for his nephew, and he had been returned to sea for a couple of months before the bailiff from the manor came to stand at George's elbow in The Plough and tell him that he had a likely candidate for the job. "Young widower from Layer-de-le-Haye; his wife was the main reason for him having a job at the Hall for she was a sempstress of some repute and Josh was found employment about the garden and house."

"He doesn't sound as if he knows much about farming."

"But he does, he comes from a farming family, and if you follow my suggestion he'll learn quickly enough."

"What would you have me do?"

The florid bailiff, with a good paunch which spoke of plenty of rich food and ale, hesitated a moment. "Well, if you ask me, it wouldn't do to rush to your mother and say that you are leaving her to follow Sam to sea — even I think you're moon-bewitched to leave dry land for that old heaving devil out yonder, and she'll have more to say on the subject than I if I'm any judge of Sarah — no, I think it'd be a good plan to meet this lad, see what you think about him, and then tell your mother that the work is getting too much for you and that if she can't see her way to paying his wages you'll have to use some of the money your uncle left for you with the solicitor in Colchester."

George regarded the bailiff. "That's sound counsel and I'll bide by it: when can Josh meet me?"

"I'll see he comes here the night after tomorrow."

★ ★ ★

George and the young widower, whom he thought must be about twenty-six or so, duly came together in the ale-house and immediately took a liking to each other. A certain sombreness in George's nature responded to the grief of the bereaved. He listened, with real sympathy, to the heartrending story of the wife's gradual decline and rapid end and told Josh something of his own loss in his father's death.

They drank two tankards of ale apiece before the real business of the meeting was broached. Josh was more eager than George could credit until he was told that the young man would have to apply for parish relief in the following week if no other occupation could be found for him.

They discussed terms and living accommodation, already a vexed question in the overcrowded farm but which Josh resolved by stating that he would fashion himself a living-space over the stable.

"You see," George explained, "except for the twins, who are the youngest of the family, all the rest are girls — five of them."

Josh lowered his eyes, and for a moment George thought he was about to have a change of heart: perhaps he found the thought of a widow and so many daughters more than he had bargained for but, after taking a deep breath, he said that he was willing to do as George wished.

Greatly relieved George asked him to come and share Sunday meat at Langetts and make the acquaintance of the Mitchells. "I need a day or two to prepare my mother," he said as they shook hands and parted company.

The cold, January night was brilliant with ice-white stars, and there was the smell of frost in the air. Good weather in which to finish off the ploughing and see to the endless repairs to shippon, pig-sties and barns: the latter being among the chief glories of Langetts, having been built before the existing house in the reign of the Tudors of weather-boarding and rich, red tiles. As a child George had liked nothing better than to help his father in the warm protection of their ancient walls. If he felt any pangs at leaving his birthplace it was for these strong, seemingly indestructible buildings.

2

THE gardens of the Château de la Bellefontaine had never looked more beautiful. The hot June sun brought out the scent of the lime blossom and from where she sat on a swing suspended from a low bough Magdalena, countess de la Bellefontaine, could hear the buzzing of countless bees hunting for nectar in the wax-like flowers. As she moved lazily back and forth she could see the distant Loire glinting amongst the foliage of the willows which bordered the great wide river. A cuckoo called from the deep woods behind her parent's house and swallows swooped low to retrieve a feast of insects.

Magdalena was exceedingly happy for today was her own and her father's fête and they were to celebrate the double anniversary of his fortieth and her fifteenth birthday with a banquet and a dance.

If this were not sufficient pleasure for

one day her beloved cousin Bastien was coming from Grenoble to join in the celebrations: the thought of this approaching joy made her almost giddy with excitement, while sensations of exquisite anticipation rose from her stomach to her breast.

She was not to know (which is probably just as well, for the knowledge might well have robbed her of her innocent charm) that she was almost as pretty as the gardens which acted as her backdrop. Her dark hair, piled high to fall in ringlets about her neck, framed an oval face of near perfection in which eyes of greenish-blue promised latent fire. She was dressed in a simple *robe de campagne* of finest lawn sprinkled with daisies embroidered in silk whose leaves vied for notice with her eyes. The hands which gently pulled the ropes of the swing were long and slender, soft to touch as the stuff of her dress, never having known more arduous labour than to make music from the gold-painted clavichord in the music-room.

Lazily watching the gardeners who were giving the last touches to the lawns and formal flower-beds nearer the house, Magdalena thought first of Bastien and then of the new gown which she was to wear for the ball: impatient to see it completed she had hopped from one foot to the other while she stood for what seemed like hours to have pins put in here and bows and ornaments placed in the most becoming position, but having seen the completed creation she was certain that the ordeals had been more worth while than she could have imagined. Had not the best dressmaker in Gien been called in by her mother, the countess, to fashion the affair? The countess had hoped for a Parisian couturier, but in these sad times it was impossible to obtain such a frivolous necessity of life and she had had to be content with local talent.

Magdalena's happiness faded somewhat at the recollection of the evil forces which were at work to overthrow the ordered serenity of her existence and willed herself to think, as she had done many times before, that the reports of violence and rebellion which came to them daily were grossly exaggerated. It was impossible to believe that the men and boys, known to her since childhood, could be incited to turn on those who had cared for and employed them all their lives. Her father was a man of liberal views, as generous with his largesse to his servants as he was to the Church and the poor who crowded the narrow streets of the nearby hilltop town of Sancerre. If his friends were sceptical of his open-handedness they did, nevertheless, praise him openly and behind his back for his care for others and promised themselves almost daily that they would emulate his good example when times were better: which, of course, they never were.

★ ★ ★

Heaving a sigh of pure sensual delight Magdalena slid off the wooden seat of the swing, and retrieving her straw hat from where she had dropped it on the grass made her way towards the wide steps of her home. The château, gleaming in the afternoon sun, looked its best as the sunlight danced on the blue-grey slates of the roof. At each corner of the low house stood a tower with small windows and a witches-hat dome while above the parapet rondels added a distinctive air of their own. The house had been built by an ancestor of the la Bellefontaines in the late seventeenth century on the site of a feudal castle which had been the stronghold of a medieval noble. This impoverished courtier had been willing enough to part with his tumbledown ruin for la Bellefontaine's gold and had departed to the wild slopes of the Alpes Maritimes where he was reported to have bought a small estate and ended his days cultivating lavender and roses for the scent trade.

La Bellefontaine, himself ennobled by the Sun King for his willing assistance in providing funds from his banking interests to build Versailles, now set about pulling down the thick walls of the fortified house and bringing architects from Paris and master masons from Italy. From the plans of the first and the genius and dedication of the second the graceful mansion took shape. The main rooms faced the river and the south, while the courtyard and reception hall fronted a circular drive and a straight approach road to the highway. In the centre of the lawn before the house a tall, imposing fountain paid tribute to the name of its owner. Although small by standards of the royal châteaux and those built by earlier courtiers of the French monarchs, the house had handsome rooms and luxurious tapestries, curtains and furniture.

Magdalena's mother, who was of the older nobility of France, was also an heiress in her own right, and she had added to the beauty of the château by buying paintings and porcelain to equal the Sèvres services in the king's palaces. On an occasion such as this evening's fête, servants had been busy weeks before in washing and polishing to make everything ready for the hundred guests who were to dance, eat and sleep beneath her roof.

Magdalena climbed the sweeping stone stairway to her bedroom. This small chamber was close by her mother's apartments and led out of her governess-turned-chaperone's plainer room. On the south-western corner of the house with a view to the river and the encroaching woods, the room was lined from ceiling to floor with silk damask and a new-fangled couch bed without bedposts. To offset this departure from time-honoured custom a small coronet had been fixed at the head and gauze curtains fell from this about the pillows like a bridal veil. A silver bath was placed in readiness in the adjoining closet, and Magdalena pulled the bell-rope to summon maids and hot water. When the shutters were closed and the bath filled the girl sent away her attendants and climbed into the scented water to dream of Bastien and wash away the fatigue of walking from the swing to the house.

★ ★ ★

In the event the long-anticipated evening was a disappointment. It was not that the sea-coloured dress did not come up to expectations, for Magdalena did not need her attendants to tell her that she had never looked more beautiful — or more grown up. For the first time her mother had allowed the neck of the bodice to be cut low enough to expose part of her bosom while whalebones helped to accent the slim line of her waist and her flat stomach; the sempstresses of Gien, it would appear, had little to learn from their Parisian counterparts.

Neither did the food, the music nor the liveliness of the company fail to please. It was, rather, some lack in herself — and in Bastien — that caused the accidie which was to haunt her for days after the event.

And she was never to forget the evening, for it marked her first meeting with the soberly dressed, strange young man from Grenoble.

To all outward appearances Bastien was as he had always been, charming, exquisitely turned out and attentive. It was this last attribute which caused the faint ruffles of disquiet in Magdalena, for if her cousin were eager to dance with her, he was just as pleased to stand up with her friends and particularly with a young widow who lived not far from her uncle's home near Amboise.

Magdalena regarded this attractive matron with an emotion which could be described as envious dislike, for the girl (she looked little more than that although rumour had it she was approaching her thirtieth birthday) had a poise which set her apart from the *jeunes filles* who anxiously awaited partners. Magdalena avoided her, the sight of her cool charms making the palms of her own hands moist and the constriction of the tight bodice almost unbearable.

The swell of her white breasts had been a cause of embarrassment in itself, for she had surprised more than one leer on the faces of her father's contemporaries: a sensation which had made her long to rush upstairs and put on one of the safer dresses hanging in her extensive wardrobe.

Bastien led her out for the first dance and all had been well until he took her to supper and she discovered that the easy camaraderie which had existed between them up until now had disappeared. The young man talked incessantly of things about which she knew nothing and bragged with blind vanity of his success with ladies of all ages and class.

"But I thought you were at the University to study," she managed to interpolate when he stopped on one occasion to take a breath.

"Oh, that," he said, airily, "*ma petite cousine*, there are more things to be learnt in life than can be gleaned from dull books."

"Doubtless," she found courage to reply, "but will not my uncle be disappointed if you fail to secure honours?"

"My father was at pains to tell me on my departure that I must learn the ways of the world as well as my lectures and, anyway, who needs to study to give orders to servants?"

A very faint chill at the base of her spine made Magdalena shudder, but she shook off the presentiment of danger and asked him to tell her more of his adventures: it was better to hear him boast than to lose him to the widow who sat not far away with her bold, dark eyes constantly upon Bastien.

It was while Magdalena was covertly regarding this odious female that she caught sight of a slim, fair-haired man deep in conversation with some of the local dignitaries her father had insisted should be invited. Unable to stop herself,

Magdalena said: "Who is that brown-suited man over there in the corner?"

Bastien stopped in full flight and turned lazily on his heel. "Oh, that's François Baron — a friend of mine from Grenoble. He's staying with us, so I had to bring him along. Would you care to meet him?"

Before she could stop him Bastien began to lead her across the crowded room to the group who talked, oblivious of their surroundings, with set faces in direct contrast to the gaiety of the rest.

"François," Bastien cried, cutting into the debate without formality, "Magdalena is dying to meet you and would take you away from this pressing debate."

As Magdalena blushed for the shame of this untrue and discourteous introduction she was regarded by her cousin's friend with a level and penetrating look. "I am enchanted to meet the daughter of our host," François said, "and if these gentlemen will excuse me I'll claim the privilege of asking her to accompany me in search of one of those delectable syllabubs I noticed."

His voice was cultured, incisive and musical. Magdalena found herself led towards the supper-table which was set out with silver bowls filled with strawberries, rich cream and pastries which were the *pièces de résistance* of her father's chef.

As Magdalena was unhappily aware of Bastien making his way towards the widow she heard him call out: "Trust François to be thinking of nothing but his stomach."

If she was expecting her new escort to take offence Magdalena was surprised to hear François laugh. "Only a fellow who has never known hunger could make a remark like that."

Magdalena raised her eyebrows and regarded him with her head on one side. "Have *you* known what it is not to have sufficient to eat?"

"Frequently, Magdalena; when one is of a family of twelve children there are many occasions on which one has gone famished to bed. A situation which I am sure has never arisen in your young life."

Magdalena drew herself up, the gesture unwittingly displaying the swell of her young bosom. "Unfortunately, monsieur,

God has chosen to take my brothers to himself before they were out of their cradles."

"Forgive me, I did not know: and yet, who knows, it may well be that we shall envy them their fate before too long."

"What do you mean by that?"

"You are not so cocooned in this rarefied atmosphere to realize that our very way of life is threatened." François stopped, "But this is your birthday and I shall not spoil it for you with sombre tales. Select one of these excellent dishes and I'll find somewhere for us to sit."

He found a table on the terrace where pitch torches flamed to keep away the insects. Beyond their raw light a full moon filled the starlit sky with luminous brilliance.

"It is hard to imagine," Magdalena mused, "that there is want anywhere in the world."

"I thought we had decided to forget the miseries of the suffering for this evening."

"It was you who brought up the subject."

"Then I apologise for troubling your pretty head."

Before she could stop, herself Magdalena said, "Do you find me pretty?"

The dark expressive eyes regarded her with that level disconcerting gaze. "Devastatingly so, but I shall do everything in my power to resist the temptation to fall in love with you for I can offer you nothing but an impoverished dukedom."

"Dukedom?" Magdalena's tone was incredulous.

"You thought that my puritanical dress could only be associated with one of the minor professions — and who could blame you? But I do assure you that when my father died and left me the care of my mother and my brothers and sisters he also bequeathed me his title and the thousand responsibilities which went with it."

"Do you take your duties so seriously?"

He parried with another question. "Does not your father do the same thing? By all accounts he is a man of charity and honour."

"*Mon père* is the kindest man in the world."

"And he dotes upon you — and who would not."

Magdalena smiled. (Afterwards she was to recall that this was the first time she had done so spontaneously.) "*Maman* is not always so pleased with me."

"Ah, but that is understandable. Mothers have a way of wishing their daughters to be perfect and the slightest sliding from grace is sufficient to warrant a fiercer attack than is deserved." He looked at her. "Tell me what you do with yourself."

"Do?" She was genuinely surprised. "Why, I play with my little dog, hunt a little, dance, play the piano and sing sometimes for Papa's friends."

"And what about studies? Do you read M. Voltaire or the plays of Molière?"

"I regret that Mademoiselle, my gov — my chaperone, finds me a trial where learning is concerned."

"That astonishes me for you have a mind which needs awakening. Where have you travelled?"

"To Paris."

"Nowhere else?"

Magdalena shook her head. "Tell me what you are doing at Grenoble."

"Fulfilling my father's last wishes and

finishing my studies."

"What are you reading?"

"Philosophy."

"But so is Bastien — or so I supposed."

"He and I attend the same *précepteur*, but Bastien, with his charm, already knows all that he requires to go forward in life." François rose abruptly. "I am monopolising your time and receiving black looks from Madame la comtesse who thinks, quite rightly, that her daughter has spent sufficient time with a dowdy, penniless nobody and should be making herself pleasant to all her other eager suitors."

"As it is my birthday I shall run the gauntlet of her displeasure and ask you to be seated once again and tell me some more of your life."

François shrugged. "There is little else to tell. Would you have me discuss the current prices our cattle and sheep are fetching at market or would you rather hear me discourse on Cicero's *De Republica*?"

"What is that?" The beautiful eyes were wide.

"You have not heard of Rome's most famous philosopher? Do not shock me by telling me that you do not read Latin?"

Magdalena could not be sure if she were being mocked, but to hide her uncertainty she looked down and shook her head.

"Then this must be remedied at once! In the morning, with my letter of thanks to your mother, will come a projected course of study that you should undertake immediately. You have access to your father's library? Well then, everything you will need will most certainly be obtainable there."

"And if I don't care to follow your advice?"

"That is your own affair — but if I have come to know you a little during our brief time together I am sure you will be curious to know what I think you should study. Am I far from the truth?"

"No, for you intrigue me, sir."

"On your travels, which I beg you make haste to make, do not forget to go to England — that garden of a country — and should you ever come to the south of your land, my estates are between Grenoble and the sea: at Castellane to be exact."

"Castellane? I shall seek it out tomorrow on the globe."

"Then with that promise I'll steal the handsome widow from your cousin so that you may end your evening happy in the arms of Bastien. For that is what you want, is it not?"

Magdalena blushed. Had she made it so obvious that her interests lay in Bastien? Yet she had not looked in his direction all the time François had been speaking to her, and had, indeed, forgotten his existence.

But she danced with him all the same, but when, shortly before cockcrow, she fell into her pretty bed her last waking thoughts were not of that handsome young dandy but of his fair and disturbing friend.

3

ATE took a kindly hand in helping George break the news of Josh's appearance at Sunday dinner. George, who had never suffered a day's illness in his life, was struck down on the morning after meeting his prospective helper with an attack of the ague. This disease was known to be fatal in the marshy countryside around Helmdon and the womenfolk hastened to bring hot possets and spare blankets from their beds to the sufferer. George rapidly recovered his strength and was well enough to attend matins with the rest of the family on the Sunday: however, his illness was sufficient excuse for him to broach the matter of needing an assistant and, somewhat to his surprise, his mother agreed to meet Josh.

"He'll not be needing any wages other than his keep, of course," she said in the flat voice which she had employed since her husband's death. "There's no money to spare as you would see only too well if you were to look in the ledgers."

George was never to know where he found the courage, but he asserted very firmly that Josh must be paid and that if the farm could not stand a hired hand then he would provide the money himself.

"You?" his mother queried, scorn giving her tone an added edge. "And where may you have found a fortune?"

"Uncle Samuel left sufficient funds with a solicitor in Colchester against just such a contingency as this."

"Samuel did?" Sarah regarded her eldest as if he had announced that he had struck gold in one of the furrows of the Great Field. "What harebrained nonsense is this that a stripling is told plans of which I am unacquainted?"

"I think Uncle Samuel was trying to protect you and help me to become the man of the family." For a moment George thought his mother was about to faint for her face went ashen and she closed her eyes as if blinded.

"There was only one man in this family," she spluttered, recovering herself.

"And I would not have you forget the fact."

For two reasons George was never to cease remembering his mother's words, but as the colour returned to her face she turned on her heel and climbed the steep stairs to the upper part of the house.

★ ★ ★

No especial preparations were made for Josh's attendance at the family table, but George noticed with a certain degree of amusement that his sisters, from the eldest to the youngest, made an attempt to look their best as they set out for church. All their clothes were homespun, but Sarah had managed to bring away a few of her possessions when she had fled the family home upon her marriage, and lace collars and cuffs had been among the hastily gathered treasures.

If anything Sarah looked plainer than usual, but George saw that she made a hasty survey of the church when they took up their places in their pew towards the back of the nave. There was no sight of Josh, and George added a prayer to his normal formalities that the widower would not disappoint him.

He need not have worried, for hardly had the family returned to the kitchen of the farmhouse than Lydia shouted that a stranger was approaching the gate. Immediately everyone, except Sarah, joined her at the paned window and took stock of the newcomer.

"Why, he's more handsome than you, George," his eldest sister noted.

"And he looks big and strong, even if his face is a little pale." The speaker received a sharp dig in the ribs, for experience had taught the family that to speak of bereavement was to put their mother into a worse humour than usual. "He's been hurrying and is out of breath," the culprit added, somewhat lamely.

"Well, open the door then and remember your manners," Sarah growled. "Let's have a sight of this paragon who is going to help George manage what one man, in his time, always saw to without aid."

Josh came into the kitchen, pulling off his knitted cap and greeting George. George led the young man to where

Sarah sat in her rocking chair close by the hearth: for a moment it appeared as if his mother were about to take one of her turns and retire to her bedroom, but after what seemed a long time she said in a clearer voice than they had heard of late, "You're not a Mitchell, are you?"

Josh laughed; a merry sound that contrasted strangely with his morose expression as he had crossed the threshold earlier. "Not that I know of, ma'am, my name's Josiah Stead and I was born in the parish of Tolleshunt D'Arcy — if that means anything to you."

"It doesn't, although my mother was wont to visit the rector's wife on occasions."

The girls exchanged glances. This was a change! Sarah was not given to making conversation and never referred to her past. Their interest was soon interrupted by Sarah who asked them what they thought they were all doing standing around when the dinner needed attention. As the girls scampered to the scullery she sent the twins to the woodshed to replenish the already blazing fire.

"Now, young man," she addressed

Josh, "George here tells me that he is in need of an extra pair of hands."

"Since you acquired that extra field on the other side of the hill I'd hazard a guess that he has his time fully occupied — and twelve head of cattle take a deal of milking and mucking out."

"I see you've studied the place."

"If I'm to be of use I must know what is involved."

"You'll not be needing wages?"

George was about to protest at this going back on his mother's part, but Josh forestalled him by saying that he would work for a month for his keep and if, at the end of that time, he proved of use he would discuss the matter further with his employer.

"And that is myself, of course," Sarah rasped.

If Josh thought anything different he had already taken sufficient stock of the situation not to voice his opinion and merely glanced at George and nodded. The girls came in with the immense willow-pattern dish on which stood the inevitable joint of underdone mutton. Lydia followed with the suet pudding, and her immediate senior, Hannah, brought in a bowl of mashed swedes. Sarah rose and took her place at the head of the scrubbed deal table. "Sit on my right hand," she commanded Josh, and as he did so she set about the business of carving.

At first all was confusion as the pudding was dissected and the plates passed from hand to hand: when all was finished an uncomfortable silence fell on the warm room which was only broken by the sound of Lydia's persistent cough and the roaring of the wind in the open chimney.

Josh broke the lull by asking the company at large if anyone played a musical instrument. Receiving denials from everyone Hannah enquired if he had skill in this direction.

"Well, I do play the violin, and if Mrs. Mitchell will allow it on the Sabbath I'd be happy to give you a tune."

"I shall be retiring to rest when the meal is finished, so you may play as you will."

Now that the ice had been broken all the family, with the exception of George, began to ask the stranger questions as to how he had acquired his skill and the instrument. Josh, it soon appeared, was anxious enough to talk about himself, and George realised that he had completely lost the woebegone expression he had worn on their first meeting in The Plough. Animation and the good food which he ate wolfishly brought colour to his cheeks, and George saw that he was quite good looking: a fact which had escaped his notice until this moment. As the eldest member of the family he knew a pang of anxiety for the safety of his brood of sisters: they were all of an age to be impressed by male company and, starved of it as they were, would be easy conquests for a predatory man.

There seemed no cause for concern at the moment, for it was the boys who were claiming Josh's attention. It transpired that he was a taxidermist and also possessed some skill at topiary.

"Taxidermist? Topiary?" Reuben asked, puzzled.

"Don't show your intolerable ignorance," Sarah snapped, "you know well enough that Josh means he can stuff wild

50

creatures and cut their shapes in garden bushes."

George, who had not known what either word meant, shuddered at the thought of the small animals scampering about the fields being displayed in glass cases such as Josh was now describing: eating rabbits was one thing, but snaring birds to imprison them to hang mute on some wall or mantel-shelf was another. He found himself not so taken with the newcomer as he had been on first acquaintance. Unnoticed he left the table and went out to the byre to look at a sick cow. The creature had had trouble with a retained placenta after calving, and although he had worked through the night to assist the sufferer he was still concerned she would die. He was startled out of his contemplation of the red and white animal by Josh's voice. "I know nothing of farm stock, Mr. George, so there'll be a lot for you to teach me."

"You'll soon learn," George commented. "By all accounts you're a quick pupil." He tried to keep the edge from his voice and hoped the other man would not notice his gruff tone.

Apparently he did not, for he asked if he might see the stable loft where he was to make his lodging. "I've a bed and a small chest, and with your permission I'll return to the Hall at Layer and fetch them with my other belongings."

"Go by all means, and perhaps one of the boys would like to go with you to give a hand."

"I've already asked them, and they're both coming."

"Well enough, but remind them that they may not set out until after they have attended Sabbath School."

"Mrs. Mitchell has already reminded them. May I be so bold to ask how long it is since your father died?"

"Two years," George replied, reluctant to discuss this matter at the moment without realising the reason.

"Your mother took it hardly?" It was more a statement than a question, and George did not comment. Josh went on, apparently not expecting any response. "And you have done very well to manage so much land and so many beasts."

"It is but a small herd and the girls

help with the milking — "

"But there goes more to managing cattle than sitting with a bucket beneath their udders. Do the boys help?"

George was indignant. "They do indeed — I see to that: but they attend dame's school in Langenhoe, and our mother considers that book-learning is as important as manual labour."

"Can you read and write?"

"I can."

"Would you teach me? My parents were not as far-seeing as yours."

"How old would you be, Josh?"

"Thirty at my next birthday."

"And when will that be?"

"March."

"You look young for your age."

"It is a family thing — my father is often mistaken for my brother."

"Is he indeed." George studied the smooth face and the innocent-seeming blue eyes. "Do you resemble him?"

"Very much so I'm told."

"He is a farmer, so I believe."

"That's true."

"Why do you not work for him?"

"I'm the youngest of the brood — and

they did not approve of my marriage."

"That seems to be common hereabouts." George spoke without thinking and wished himself dumb for betraying his dead father.

"Oh — and of whom would you be thinking?"

"A couple I know who live not so far away." The lie sounded obvious, even in his own ears, but Josh seemed to accept the statement, and they went together to inspect the loft.

★ ★ ★

During the next weeks there were to be many occasions on which George wished that the bailiff had found him other help, but he realised Josh took a great deal off his shoulders and no task was too distasteful or heavy for him to undertake. In the fields, especially when the sleet was whipping their cheeks raw, he was competent, and he excelled in turning the earth to prepare the vegetable plot for the summer crops. Working with the cows it was obvious that he had not been used to the job and he was inclined to lose his temper if the beasts did not behave as he thought they should. Yet he sat one entire night at George's side to help in tending the sick cow.

But it was in the house George found most to dislike. Never had he seen such a profusion of tempting dishes, polished furniture and clean collars. It was as if each girl vied with the other for notice.

The greatest transformation was in the mistress of Langetts. When Josh had brought out his violin on the first evening of his coming to the farm Sarah had been in her bedroom: this was not to be the case hereafter. She lingered by the hearth when the supper platters and mugs had been washed and put out on the dresser and closed her eyes. Josh had hesitated to play when he saw her apparently preparing to doze, but she had impatiently bidden him tune up and begin. For his part George found the music unbearably disturbing, for he had never heard such melodies as the new hand drew from the fiddle. It came flowing out so that George had visions of white-sailed yachts breasting aquamarine waters in a land of perpetual summers. Where did they come from, these pictures of his mind? Not from the old City at West Mersea where the smugglers' narrow boats rubbed cheeks with the sturdy fishing-craft nor yet in Brightlingsea where he had once been with Uncle Samuel and his father in the far-off days of his childhood. What magic lay in Josh's sturdy fingers that he could conjure the stuff of dreams?

What mirages did his sisters see? What yearnings were aroused in the thoughts of his young brothers? Did they, perhaps, have fancies which beckoned them away from Langetts with this unbearable longing which threatened George's very existence? He grew more despondent as the days passed, for he realised that it would take longer than he had anticipated to bring Josh to the point where he would be able to confront his mother with the fact that he was joining Samuel as a seafarer. This was not because of the older man's shortcomings but some sense of responsibility George felt towards the farm and the memory of his father. If Josh had a fault it was, perhaps, that he was too eager to please, too quick to grasp and put into practice a new idea. Then having established that he could perform a given task he lost interest in the project and had to be reminded that it required doing day in, day out, until one season changed into the next.

★ ★ ★

Spring came with a burst of bird-song and a premature breaking of leaves on the winter-bare trees. Josh announced that he would like to spend his first wages on a supper party for the family. George glanced at his mother when this idea was mooted over a Sunday dinner table but found that she was not going to forbid the affair as he had anticipated: celebrations were taboo at Langetts since her husband's death.

Now she merely enquired: "And when is your birthday?"

"The seventeenth of this month, ma'am."

"St. Patrick's day, if I'm not mistaken, so there'll be double cause to keep the occasion. We'll kill a goose and I'll make a fruit pudding."

If the rest were as astonished as George was they showed nothing but excitement at the prospect and fell to discussing the problem of whether or not they had sufficient time to finish the dresses they were making from the silks Samuel had given them.

But Josh had not finished yet. "And what do you say, ma'am, to asking some of the fellows I meet in The Plough of an evening to come and join us? Surely 'tis time the lot of them were allowed to show their pretty faces somewhere else than in church of a Sabbath?"

Sarah returned to her former manner and remarked in a grim voice that there was plenty of time for her daughters to meet suitable men and that the feast would be strictly a family affair. George forgot about the business, for he was totally occupied in finishing the sowing and seeing to the hedges and ditches. The February rains had filled the latter with broken branches, stones and old bird's nests, and he and Josh were out in the changeable weather until dark clearing and trimming.

The others were not as remiss as he,

and on the evening of the seventeenth he came in from changing in the shed to find new candles in brass holders burning on the table and the best china which his father had scraped and saved to give Sarah on their last wedding anniversary before his death laid ready for use. A fat goose, not from the farm, was being turned on the spit by Reuben while other delicious smells came from the peel oven in the corner of the chimney breast. Of the girls and his mother there was no sign.

"When will supper be ready?" he asked.

Reuben shrugged. "When Josh comes in from the loft, I suppose; it is *his* birthday. I only hope when it comes to mine the same fuss is made."

"Where are the girls?"

"Dressing, if you ever heard of such rubbish. What do they think they are — the gentry?"

"And our mother?"

"Oh, she's in her room; probably got one of her sick headaches. I shouldn't be surprised as she's been in the kitchen best part of the day." He yelped as a spurt of hot fat dropped on to his hand. While he licked it off George went out to the barn, taking a lantern in his hand; he was famished but refused to kick his heels waiting for a feast never accorded him on his birthdays.

★ ★ ★

When he did return to the kitchen it was to find all assembled and preparing to sit without him. The girls were so changed that he had difficulty in realising which was which. The elder two had piled their hair in chignons and the others had contrived ringlets to fall on bare shoulders in a manner George had seen on his monthly market visits to Colchester when the quality had been going in and out of The George opposite the stalls.

Moving among the brightly clad females was an older woman in a gown of tawny satin, her head bare and her cheeks and lips touched with colour so that her eyes glowed. It took George several seconds to realise that the apparition he saw was his mother.

4

NOT a month after Magdalena's birthday party the simmering unrest in the country of France, which had been the cause of the grave and urgent discussions which had taken place that night, erupted into the taking of the Bastille.

A Parisian mob, consisting of the unemployed and the hopeless swelled by trouble-mongers, sympathetic artisans and shop assistants, stormed its way into the old fortress on the east side of the city and forced the governor, Bernard Jordan, marquis de Launday, to surrender the keys. When he did so he was ruthlessly pushed on one side and orders were given for the drawbridge to be lowered. A screaming mob stampeded the building and released the prisoners: that these numbered but seven men (two of them madmen) meant nothing to the insurgents, and the attack upon the ancient stronghold became a signal for the overthrow of what the rebels thought of as tyranny.

Moderate aristocrats, like Magdalena's father, held hurried meetings to decide what to do if the local peasantry copied the example of their brothers in Paris. As they made up their minds to be tolerant it became obvious that Louis XVI and his wife, Marie Antoinette, had been forced to relinquish the reigns of government which now rested with the people.

In the privacy of their own salon the count and the countess of la Bellefontaine debated the problem of their young and beautiful daughter.

"I am certain," said the count, "that we should send Magdalena away to England or Naples while there is still time."

"Time?" his wife queried. "Pah, what is this but the rising of a few serfs who will soon be put in their place by the army."

"My dear, I very much regret that you have not a full grasp of the situation. I wish, with all my heart, that you were right, but to my mind the events in Paris have triggered off something which could well end up in destroying our world as we know it."

"But how can that be? The madmen who are holding the king are ignorant, unarmed and lawless."

"Lawless they may be but neither uneducated nor without guns: contrary to your beliefs the army is not altogether loyal, and you forget that France has a system of schooling whereby the poorest can learn to read and write."

"More's the pity. If they were kept where they should be, working in the fields and vineyards, they'd have no time for reading the works of traitors like Voltaire."

"It is impossible to govern a country where the majority are underfed and badly housed. You must remember also that the present king is not even a shadow of Louis XIV — he has no sense of progress or vision for the future. The situation we have now would never have existed in the time of the Sun King."

"Why did someone not warn Louis?"

"Jacques Necker tried to do so and all he received for his pains was dismissal."

"But he has been reinstated."

"True, and now works the will of the Third Estate rather than that of the monarch." The count walked to the window and looked out to the river, gleaming through the trees: he had been born in the room above, and he loved his home for its air of abiding security as much as for its elegance and rich possessions. He knew that he would have been just as happy in whatever station of life he had been brought up, but he knew also that his wife was more narrow in her outlook and craved the luxury with which she was surrounded. "Where *is* Magdalena?" he asked. "At one time she was always to be seen riding about the fields or sitting on the swing."

"She has been very quiet since her fête day — have you not noticed?"

"I knew that she came to me to ask if M. le curé could come from his house each day to instruct her in Latin and geography." The count turned to his wife. "Is that where she is now? In the library with Fourré?"

"Most probably: Mamselle tells me that she works each morning for two hours at her books. What does she hope to gain by filling her head with such nonsense?"

"She is probably wiser than we know. You won't make any effort to stop her, will you?" As his wife shrugged he went on to say that they were still not coming to a decision about their daughter's future. "Do you not feel that it would be better to go away?"

"I am adamant! No grubby, smelly peasant is going to frighten me away from my heritage — I'll take a gun to him sooner than move from here."

* * *

So, for the moment the matter was dropped. For some time it appeared that the countess was right in her judgement, and although other parts of France were terrorised by bands of rampaging labourers the fair lands surrounding the Loire went free. By the end of August 'The Great Fear' which gripped the aristocracy began to subside and the moderates on both sides of the opposing forces seemed to be in control.

★ ★ ★

At Christmas Bastien returned from Grenoble and came to visit his cousin. Magdalena sprang up with delight when he was announced, managing to suppress the pang of disappointment she felt when she realised that François was not with him.

"How has my enchanting *cousine* fared during these momentous days?" he asked as he kissed her first on one cheek and then on the other.

"I've been so busy that I've not had time to worry about the troubles in the rest of the country."

A servant brought coffee and cognac, and when he had departed Bastien stretched out his tall frame on the chair opposite Magdalena at the hearth. "So busy? At what — your embroidery?" The mocking note in his voice made Magdalena bridle.

"You asked me if I had fared well during 'The Great Fear' and the disturbing news from Paris — it might interest you to know that I've been studying with M. le curé in an attempt to understand what lies behind the unrest which has caused the king's subjection."

Bastien regarded her, his head on one side. "*Hélas*, what is the world coming to when a pretty woman begins to think for herself! If this state of affairs is allowed to continue we shall have women in government and who knows what else — "

Magdalena cut him short. "Have you not read — or heard, at least — that it is the women who are the most demanding in their threats to established order? What do you think has brought that about?"

"Not reading, my sweet, that's for certain: the rabble of Paris and other cities speak from empty bellies rather than cultured minds."

"Then you have compassion for them?" Magdalena was surprised and hoped her voice did not echo her sentiment.

"Of course, all conscientious people must be sorry for those who suffer in a way that we cannot understand. François says — "

"François? François says what?"

Bastien regarded her yet more intently, and with infuriating deliberation raised his quizzing glass to his eye. "Methinks, *mon ami, le duc* has replaced your humble servant in your affections."

"How can that be so? You and I've been friends since the cradle!"

"Stranger things have been known, Magdalena — and François is a devilish attractive fellow even if he hasn't the slightest idea of dressing himself properly."

"He hasn't the money to wear anything but sober clothes!" Magdalena retorted.

"As I said, you seem to know a great deal about the studious young gentleman, and that brings to mind the object of my call this day."

"Which was not to see me?" The brilliant eyes were wide open: no woman likes to think that a man comes to a house without she being the reason behind the visit.

"Ah, but what else would bring me here?" Bastien teased. "My purpose was threefold — to invite you and your esteemed parents to a very sober and modified celebration of what might well be our last New Year upon earth, to see you and to deliver a letter from a certain impoverished nobleman."

Maddeningly Bastien hummed a tune as he pretended to search in his pockets. At last he found what he searched for and handed over the sealed missive with a little bow. Although she thanked him coolly and allowed the letter to lie upon her lap Magdalena was burning to read its contents. Instead she asked Bastien to tell her about the University and the effect of the revolution upon the students.

Once launched upon this topic nothing seemed likely to prevent her cousin from talking for hours, and a servant came to summon them to dine with the important document still unread. With a grace which she found difficult to assume Magdalena followed Bastien into the *salle à manger*.

It was to be nightfall before she was able to escape to the haven of her room and tear open the seal.

'Dear and lovely countess,' she read, 'I am taking the opportunity of Bastien's return to his native *pays* to send you a list of books you might find interesting. I know that you have been following the advice which I had the temerity to inflict upon you at your birthday fête from the note which you sent me. I must confess that I was overjoyed to have won you round to my way of thinking and only hope that you will take my advice on the other subject of our discussions. My elder brothers have departed to Naples and four of the girls are in England — only my two young brothers and the other sisters remaining at Castellane to help in the running of the estate. I am trying, very hard, to follow my self-imposed discipline that I should not fall in love with you, but admit that I am not having a great deal of success. Perhaps now that I have left Grenoble I shall have sufficient to do with the farm and keeping a balance between loyal tenants and those influenced by the turn of events in Paris. You know that I am and shall remain your faithful servant, and you can believe, dear Magdalena, that if I — or my poor dwelling — can be of service to you and yours you have but to send word. François.'

This was the first love-letter (if that was what it was) Magdalena had received, and she hugged the thought of it while she read the works François had recommended and while she and the rest of the family made a brave effort to attend Mass on Christmas Day and see in the New Year with no show and a cheerful face upon a dark situation.

★ ★ ★

At about the same time in the village of Helmdon in the county of Essex a very different war of attrition was being waged.

By now Josh had settled in to Langetts as if he had never known another home. The young man had remedied his shortcomings with the livestock and now was as efficient in the shippon as he had been all along in the fields and meadows. He had lost the hangdog expression which had touched the sympathetic side of George's nature, and he bloomed with a health which filled out his emaciated frame and gave his cheeks a bronzed glow of health. George grudgingly admitted to himself that the unhappy creature who had come to his home was now a most presentable man. As far as George could judge he showed no favour to any of the girls, treating them all the same in a fraternal manner, as ready to criticise as he was to banter or pay a rare compliment. To the mistress of the house he paid an almost deferential respect: probably learnt while he was in domestic service. George was not certain if his mother responded or not to this treatment, for since the day of Josh's feast she had stayed in her accustomed chair to listen to the fiddle-playing and had retired to bed as soon as Josh laid aside the instrument. Nor had she put on again the tawny-coloured dress nor touched her face with colour, yet she was altered in some way which was indefinable to her eldest son. George paid her scant attention, for Josh forestalled him, and the hurt she had inflicted upon him since his father's death went too deep for hope of easement. If the girls saw any change in her they were more occupied with the business of finding favour with the new hand than in giving heed to

Sarah. When she spoke to George it was in her customary hectoring way, and she did not once praise him for the extra money he brought back from market or give him the satisfaction of knowing she was pleased that he had someone to assist in the working of the farm. If anything she spent more time in her own room than before and was frequently in bed when George climbed the steep stairs to his shared bedquarters.

George had other problems beside the decision as to when he should quit Langetts; he knew he delayed until he had news from Uncle Samuel who was at present on a voyage to bring sugar from the West Indies.

It was Bess who caused him to have sleepless nights, for his relationship with her had developed to the point when she was claiming an engagement ring or some other token as his visible promise of future marriage. He had been driven into deeper sexual experiences with her than he had intended mainly through the unhappiness of his home life. At least, in the safe haven of the stable loft at The Plough, he was able to forget for an hour or two his other worries. Bess was comfortable, pretty and lusted after by most of the village men. She gave of her charms with hearty good humour and was usually cheerful and compliant.

As Christmas neared, however, she had shown the true nature of her feelings towards George by refusing him anything beyond a snappish peck or two and stating that he would get nothing further until she was assured that his intentions were honourable.

"You know, well enough, I've no means to marry you," he told her, sitting with his knees hunched to his chin, his face set with misery.

"Then you've no right to have lain with me in the straw."

"How do I know you haven't done the same with all the men in the inn who make sheeps' eyes at you?"

"Because I say so."

George made an attempt to pull her down into the straw, his hands fumbling at the bodice of her dress, but if he were strong for his eighteen years she was lithe and she sprang away from him and went away down the ladder.

A week later she told him she was expecting their child. George went cold with fear; a sensation which made the pit of his stomach like ice-cold water and his knees ready to give way beneath him. "How do you know?" he managed to splutter.

"How else, of course, than by the usual signs. Surely I don't have to explain those to you?" Later George lay tossing and turning on the narrow pallet in his bedroom. The wind howled across the marshes and a melancholy owl hooted from the roof of the barn: although it was a wild night and the sea would be lashed to fury he would gladly have exchanged the relative peace of his bedroom for the cot of a merchantman. If only Samuel would come home and put him out of his misery.

He was interrupted in his abject despondency by the banging of the outer back door. Cursing he climbed from under the blanket and naked went downstairs to investigate. To his surprise the door was unlatched and swinging on its hinges; he was certain that he had bolted it as usual when he had come to bed, and, lighting a taper, he explored the kitchen and the sheds looking for an intruder. It was not unknown for marshmen to take unasked-for shelter in the houses about the creeks and inlets, and smugglers pursued by Excise officers were known to seek sanctuary without invitation from any of the houses who had reason to be grateful for their past assistance.

Finding all in order George went back to bed and fell asleep: his last thought being that his own mind was becoming unhinged with Bess, his mother's continuing opposition and the non-appearance of Samuel.

He was relieved of his worry concerning Bess by a chance encounter with the bailiff. The older man came into The Rose of Peldon where George had gone to drink one Saturday night in order to avoid being with Josh and joined George as he warmed himself by the roaring ingle-nook fire.

"Well," he said, "I suppose we must expect cold weather at this time of year but I don't remember a vicious winter such as this since I was a lad."

"What'll you drink?" George asked.

"Can you run to a tot of rum since you've taken on an extra hand?" When George nodded and brought the beaker of spirit he asked: "Is the fellow still helping you?"

"Aye, you did not fail me in your choice."

"You don't sound as if you are entirely happy with him, all the same."

George shrugged. "We rub along well enough."

"He hasn't seduced any of your sisters yet?"

"He has not — and better not try, either. I'll kill him if he lays a finger on any one of them."

The bailiff glanced at him and, sizing up the set mouth and the set of the cleft chin, changed the subject. "Have you heard about Bess at The Plough?"

George's expression, if anything, became more disgruntled. "What about Bess?" he growled.

"Old farmer Twyman — you know, the widower over by the Colchester road — has got her in the family way." The bailiff chuckled. "Her parents are demanding weddings and finery and the lot: that should teach the old fellow not to go eyeing tempting young maidens."

A delicious warmth of relief began to percolate through George's veins until a smile touched his mouth for the first time in days. All he said was: "Good luck to the poor old devil and I hope he has joy of the match. Will you have another rum? I could do with one before the walk home."

They walked the narrow lane together, the easterly wind bringing the salt air to their nostrils. George felt like dancing, and it was all he could do to stop himself giving a hop and a skip. "Thank God. Thank God," he found himself repeating until he and the bailiff parted company and he made his way up the farm-track oblivious of the deep ruts and the ice-filled puddles. He was happier than he had been for months. If only Samuel would come he could start on his new life and forget all about Langetts and his perpetual struggle to feed the hungry mouths of his family.

Throwing off his clothes he made a hasty toilet in the freezing water on the wash-stand and fell into bed. He was asleep in an instant.

He awoke to hear creaking noises coming from the direction of his mother's bedroom. Stupefied with sleep and the unusual amount of rum he had drunk in silent thanksgiving for his release from Bess' clutches he thought at first that he was hearing a repetition of the backdoor banging of the other night, but as his head cleared he knew that the sounds came from closer at hand. He lay, stiff with revulsion and horror, as he recognised the noise he had heard so often in his father's lifetime.

Had Sarah a secret lover? Was he blind that he had failed to notice some liaison between her and one of the villagers? In an instant he was out of bed, pulling on his clothes with haste, his first impulse to throw open the door of his mother's room and demand an explanation. Some sixth sense warned him that this would be an unbearable experience, and he put on the warm outer coat he had thrown carelessly on a stool and with infinite caution so that he did not rouse his sleeping brothers, stole to the door and opened it. He would wait until dawn if need be to see who violated the memory of his father and made his mother little better than a whore.

He grew cold and stiff in the limbs with waiting, but his vigil was made more necessary by the low laughs and the intimate inaudible voices he heard from beyond his mother's door. He shifted from one foot to the other keeping himself awake by sheer effort of will. The night grew very still, and from the yard he heard the first cockcrow: whoever was wantoning with Sarah — if he were a countryman — would be soon departing.

Whisperings confirmed his suspicions, and he drew back slightly into the shelter of his own doorway just in time to see a figure emerge against the soft candlelight on the night-table. There was something oddly familiar in the brief outline of the man who moved noiselessly to the head of the stairs. Restraining himself from pushing him down the polished steps George followed his quarry, moving as quietly as the intruder, crossing the kitchen behind him and picking up one of the heavy brass candlesticks from the table as he did so. He waited until the man slipped the bolt of the outer door with accustomed ease and went out into the cold morning. Coming up behind him George hit him behind the ear and had the satisfaction of hearing his quarry slump to the hard ground without a murmur. Trembling with the effort and the ordeal of his hours-long wait George hurried into the kitchen and, taking down the lanthorn, lit it from the embers of the kitchen fire. Holding it in his hand he returned to the yard and looked down on the man he had knocked senseless.

With a sickening shock of disgust he saw that it was Josh.

In a second he knew what he must do. Determination giving him courage, he found his boots in the outhouse. With shaking fingers he laced them and put on his sheepskin jacket. Past caring about the moral issues of what he was doing he found the tea-caddy where the market money was kept and filled the leather pouch which he always carried with him to Colchester. This accomplished he closed the door silently behind him, stepped over the recumbent form of his mother's lover and walked out of Langetts.

He would go to sea without the assistance of Uncle Samuel or anyone else.

5

AFTERWARDS George was not to recall much of his walk into Colchester. His brain was clouded by the thought of his mother's degradation and Josh's infamous treatment of her and her house. All the resentment which had, for so long, seethed in the deep recesses of his unconscious thought came bubbling to the surface to make him insensible to the intense cold and unseeing of the familiar landmarks along the way.

The city was already astir with farm-carts bringing eggs and chickens to market and shopkeepers opening up in preparation for the day's business. George stumbled down the cobbled street, passed the castle to the quay. For an hour he walked the Hythe looking for a ship which might be that of his uncle, but in vain.

At length he went into an inn and drank a large tankard of mulled ale: after a glance at his face the inn-keeper stopped pressing him to take some bread and cheese and left the surly-looking young man to his own devices. In a corner by himself George put back his head against the settle and fell asleep.

He was roused by the end of a knobbed stick pressing into his ribs and a rough voice telling him to stand up and look lively. George was awake and on his feet in an instant: his first fear that these men towering between him and the door were Runners and they wanted him for murdering Josh. A closer inspection told him they were press-men. His one desire was to go to sea, but he would be damned if he would enter the Service under force. Summoning every ounce of strength and will-power he flung himself between his importuners and ran for the door: years of hard toil stood him in good stead as he raced down the quayside and threw himself over a low wall.

He landed in the yard of a shipbuilder and saw a shed standing back from the entrance. He was inside the building and scaling the ladder to the loft before anyone working below had caught a glimpse of him. Moving softly and nimbly like a cat he hid himself behind a collection of tarpaulins and strained his ears for any sound of his pursuers.

George knew little of the press-gangs but what he had heard in the village, and he could not assess if they were in sufficient earnest to carry on their search. After a half an hour of cramped restriction he came to the conclusion that some other unfortunate had been impressed, and he left the security of the covering sheets to descend to the ground.

When challenged by a baize-aproned man to state his business with the yard, George replied that he was seeking work on a ship. "Ye'll not find any here — ask at Hayman's office further down the quay; they're always short of hands for their barges."

Grateful to be so easily released George touched his forehead with his knuckle and, squaring his shoulders, strode off in the direction the man had indicated.

Hayman's office proved to be a weather-boarded hut sadly in need of a coat of stain or paint. A small, bespectacled man looked up when George knocked on the door and bade him enter.

"What can I do for you?" he asked.

"I heard you are looking for hands."

"And if I am?"

"I'd be willing to offer myself."

The small man leaned back in his seat and regarded George with a scrutiny which made him want to back away. "You look strong enough, but how do I know you can work?"

"I've worked since I was eight or so in the fields and am used to being out in all weathers."

"Do you know anything about ships?"

"My father's farm was near the island of Mersea and I've often been out with his friends." It was not necessary to state that his main experience of going to sea was in a duck-punt.

"If you're suitable why do you want to quit the land?"

George hesitated: which of many reasons should he give this undersized employer? "I want to make a better life for myself," he supplied finally.

"And you think you can do that by taking to the sea?" The irony was not lost on George, but he nodded agreement. "You can't read or write, of course." It was a statement rather than a question.

"As a matter of fact I can do both."

"You can? And where, may I ask, did you learn those gentlemanly arts?"

"At home." As soon as he said the words George regretted them: he was giving away too much of his background, but the man was asking him another question.

"And what is your name?"

George thought quickly. "Gates." This was his grandmother's maiden name and sufficiently disused to be connected by outsiders with his family but associated enough in his own mind to be remembered and answered to.

There was silence, and George imagined that he was about to be dismissed when the little man rose from his desk and pulled out the top drawer of a chest at the back of the office. "It so happens that I'm looking for an apprentice mate on one of our vessels plying between here and the Dutch ports: the pay's poor but you'll learn the trade and earn yourself a chance to become a master someday. How old are you?"

"Eighteen last April."

"The ship's at the end of the quay; I'll take you to Captain Walker myself."

George's first impression of Thomas Walker was one of dismay; the master was finishing his breakfast as Hayman ushered him into his day cabin. The place reeked of stale smoke and raw spirits, and Walker, who was thick set and florid, gave the impression of not having shaved for a week, nor washed himself nor his clothing. When he looked up, however, at the sound of the owner's voice, his bright blue eyes denied the unfavourable impression, for they were kindly, shrewd and sparkling with suppressed humour. George sensed that here was a man who had come to terms with life, and despite certain failings understood himself sufficiently to retain an equable outlook upon life in general. It was obvious that he applied the same rules to other people: he did not like or admire Hayman but recognised that he was his employer and was prepared to do his bidding — as far as he judged right and necessary.

"'Morning, Mr. Hayman," he said, rising and indicating a chair. "Care for a tot this bitter morn?"

"You know I never touch the stuff," Hayman replied.

"Of course, of course, how stupid of me. A cup of chocolate?"

"Very welcome." Hayman turned to George. "This young'un wants a berth; thought he might do to replace the apprentice mate who went missing."

Walker looked full at George who stood motionless behind Hayman. "Know anything about the sea?"

This was no time to lie. "Very little, but I'm willing to learn."

"Probably, but can you read and write?"

"Yes."

"You reply — yes, sir, when you address me," Walker said without raising his voice. "Shall I test him out, Mr. Hayman?"

"By all means."

A thin child of about the same age as George's twin brothers came into the cabin at this moment. "Bring hot chocolate for Mr. Hayman, boy, and don't slop it all over the deck when you do." He did not ask George if he were hungry or thirsty. Instead he produced a sheet of paper and a mug full of quills. "Take your pick." He waved George to the only other seat in the small cabin. "Read this and make comments upon it — then sign your name."

George took the document which he saw was a list of Company rules and regulations: very restrictive, they were, all the same, straightforward. Finishing the ten or so clauses George wrote, in the bold hand which his mother had taught him, that the rules were hard but fair. He was about to sign the statement when he remembered that his name was now changed. More slowly than usual for the first time in his life he wrote — George Gates.

"Hm," Walker said, picking up the piece of paper. "There goes more to you than your clodhopping appearance would suggest. Boy, bring another mug of chocolate and a piece of yesterday's loaf."

George understood that he was accepted. Later, when Hayman had departed, he was recalled to the master's cabin.

"Now, Gates — or whatever your name is — " George blushed and looked quickly at the master — "you don't have to tell me your real name: anyone who writes as fluently as you do and hesitates when it comes to the signature *must* be remembering the pseudonym he had but recently taken as his own. You don't have to tell why you came to sea in a hurry for it's none of my business, other than to ensure that the Excise are not on your tail — they aren't, are they?" George shook his head. "Well, Gates, you tell me you're used to hard work and I'll not disbelieve you, looking at those hands, but don't think because you see me sitting at ease in here that I'm not a hard taskmaster at sea. You'll not be slacking when the mate, Mr. Benson, is about either, nor the bosun, come to think about it, but if your romantic notion of coming to sea is backed with a real desire to succeed you'll discover the life has its compensations. As you're neither fish, flesh, fowl nor good red herring you'd better make your quarters in the cuddy along of the cabin-boy. And, may I suggest, when you've sluiced yourself down you buy some more suitable clothing from shops?"

"Do I have to go ashore to do that?"

The bright eyes regarded George. "You *are* running away from something. What is it — got some girl into trouble?" George felt his face crimson, but Walker went on with a tinge of delighted malice: "Yes, you do have to go ashore but the shop's only across the path. I'll send Luke, the boy, with you for protection."

George laughed, the sound strange in his ears. "I'll go alone, thank you — sir."

"Have you money or do you want an advance?"

"I have a shilling or two," George replied, remembering the rifling of the family savings.

"Right, then get ashore. Come back here after you've eaten for I warrant you're so green that you don't know a sextant from a chart."

★ ★ ★

Later, in his rough new clothes of unbending serge and hairy wool George was given a tour of the ship by Luke. He did not need the boy to tell him that the master was a stickler for order on his ship, for the clean decks, the well-furled sails and the neatly coiled ropes told their own story.

Luke was obviously enjoying showing off his knowledge of matters nautical and George learnt that the vessel was a barque, her name was *Rosalie* and she carried a crew of twenty.

"We carry baize cloth, mostly, from here to Amsterdam, and when we can get it we bring back a cargo of spices and fruit from the East."

"Is it difficult to trade with the Lowlands?"

"Aye — and with France, too; although even in time of war contraband seems no problem."

George said nothing, realising that he was abysmally ignorant about anything beyond the hedges of Langetts: it was not unlikely that this boy already knew more about the sea than his head would ever absorb. Thinking of his home brought a vivid picture of Josh sprawled across the kitchen doorway. George was not certain if he hoped he had killed him or not: the thought of him lying with his mother in his father's place was enough to make his hands itch to be at the man's throat. How could he have abused the hospitality of the farm to take advantage of Sarah? And yet the low voices and the murmurs of pleasure which he had overheard did not sound as if the mistress of Langetts was resentful of her treatment at Josh's hands — rather to the contrary. With an audible grunt of disgust George pushed the matter from him and concentrated on the spate of information which Luke was handing out.

★ ★ ★

George ate a meal of greasy stew with his new crew-mates in the cramped quarters below decks. After a probing catechism into his background and antecedents it appeared that he was, more or less, acceptable. Remembering the master's description of himself George only told the men with whom he would now be working that he was a farmhand and tired of his occupation as such.

"It remains to be seen how soon you tire of this life," one bearded seaman commented. "Apprentices don't last above a voyage or two at most."

"Things aren't as bad as they were when I was a lad," an older man put in. "Owners and masters, for that matter, take heed of the mutiny on old Bligh's ship."

"Aye, and they better, for the ale-houses are full of talk about copying the Frenchies and taking the law into our own hands."

"But you'd never fall in with the French way, surely?" George asked.

"No knowing what we'd do if it came to it," a red-capped Irishman said. "The landowners and the squires with their stuck-up wives and daughters have had it their way too long. It's time they found out what it is to have an empty belly and starving children."

The older man prodded gently. "In every port, eh, Paddy?"

Paddy chuckled, and with a complete change of humour asked George if he would come ashore with the rest.

"Not this evening."

"'Fraid the Runners might be out?" The voice was smooth, but the green eyes under the red headgear were mischievous.

"Something like that, but I've to go to the master's cabin."

"He's soon got your nose to the grindstone, but don't worry we'll show you the sights of Amsterdam when we come there."

* * *

The captain's cabin had undergone a drastic change since George had left it some hours before. Open portholes had cleared away the mingled fumes of tobacco and gin, while brooms and polish had removed dust and marks on the desk and sea-chest. The master had followed his own advice to his new apprentice and shaved and changed his clothing: he looked quite different from the slovenly man who had interviewed George.

"Sit down, boy, sit down," he said, indicating a fixed chair opposite. "Now, navigation — to put it briefly — is the art and science of conducting a vessel safely between two points. You might think I'm talking simple truths and you're right, to a degree, but to arrive at a specified destination it is necessary to be able to find your way there, avoid entangling with other ships en route and using your sails to the best advantage so that you keep a reasonable time." He looked at George, squinting through his spectacles. "D'you understand what I'm driving at?"

"I think so — sir."

"Then take a look at this chart; it plots the course of the Colne downstream past Wivenhoe and the island of Mersea to the open sea at the mouth of the Blackwater. Damned narrow it is, too, and if the wind remains in the north-east we shall be in luck. Can you make head or tail of the thing?"

"I think so," George replied, his forehead creased with concentration. "The figures mark the depth?"

"They do, they do, but in fathoms mind; none of your land-lubber's feet and inches."

"And how long is a fathom, sir?"

Walker spread his arms wide. "About that, six feet, near enough. Now, do you know the names of the sails?"

"Mainsail, mizzen and — er — "

George's voice faltered and died away.

"Hm," Walker snorted, "for one who professed a life-long ambition to go to sea you seem to have a profound lack of knowledge of the tools of the trade. Two sails out of a possible thirty will not get you or the ship very far; here's a list and I want it word-perfect by the morning; and watch you don't set fire to the lot of us when you light the midnight oil."

George went away, reeling with exhaustion from lack of sleep, but clutching the list and a very old, soiled chart. Before he closed his heavy eyes he had the sails by heart, and from what Luke had showed him had a vague idea of where each one was placed in the maze of complicated rigging above *Rosalie*'s decks. George was always to be grateful to Thomas Walker for the advice he gave him that cold winter night and for the training which he received aboard the *Rosalie*.

As the master had said the mate, Benson, was a hard taskmaster and the bosun a foul-mouthed womaniser who was lazy into the bargain but could find the correct position for the ship's wheel from the smell of the wind.

From these three men George learnt a great deal. When he was sent up the mast and out into the rigging to help unfurl a sail and fumbled the job it was Benson who climbed behind him and put the matter right. If George had been in awe of the man before, he now admired him for not being too proud to implement his own instructions; it did not occur to him until much later that he had probably saved George's life into the bargain, for a wrongly set sail had a lash that could have sent him plummeting to the sea or the hard deck below.

The bosun taught him to have a healthy respect for the men of this world who talk a great deal and do as little as possible, for he discovered that the type could be vicious, and one's character was sooner lost by a stray word than made.

But it was Walker who was his chief mentor. From the beginning they had established some kind of rapport, and when the master found that George was as enthusiastic after three voyages as he had been before the first he devoted a good deal of his leisure in training him.

The fact that he remained aboard the

vessel was a constant source of amazement to those hands who themselves signed on for further crossings. The Irishman and the old seaman now accepted him as one of themselves, stopped taking a large portion of his food and accepted the incredulous situation of an apprentice-mate staying the course. They agreed to overlook the hours which George spent studying for what they frankly regarded as a waste of time and were happy to take him along to the low haunts of Amsterdam and other ports in the Lowlands.

At first George was titillated by the demonstrations which fascinated his crew-mates, but after a while he found that the erotic displays of half-naked females began to pall. Uncertain of how to free himself without causing offence to the rest George began to drink more heavily than he had ever done before. One night, lying in his cot while the ship was in the dock of S. Ryk's at Amsterdam, he fell asleep over a book of navigation: his arm dropped across the candle he had foolishly placed beside him and in seconds his sleeve was alight.

Fortunately for him, Luke, dismissed by Captain Walker for the evening, came in before the fire took the bedding, but his screams brought the master to the cubby. George awoke from fuddled sleep to find Walker glaring down at him, all humour erased from his blue eyes. "You young fool! D'you realise you couldn've been the death of us all? Put yourself to rights and come to my cabin."

On deck a bucket of cold water brought some sense to George's aching head, and a hurried change into his only other clothing brought a small measure of something approaching order. Pale with apprehension and sick to the pit of his stomach he made his way to the dressing-down he richly deserved.

In the event he was confined to the punishment quarters below the water-line where he was inaugurated into the skills of baiting traps for the rats which infested the cramped and ill-smelling bilges. Two days of this was sufficient to put him off drink for ever — although, rather naturally, it did not.

He was called to the master's cabin an hour or two before the barque was due to sail for home. "Close the door," Walker said, "and give me an explanation — if you can."

Haltingly, painfully conscious of the burns on his forearm, George talked about his visits ashore and his indulgence in the cheap spirits which were readily available to the seamen at any port.

"You're not a puritan," Walker said, "but you're sickened by the company your mates keep, is that it?"

"Something like that."

"And you drink too much because you're not strong enough to tell the others why you don't want to go ashore with them."

"When you live with men — " George's voice trailed.

"Ah, yes, there's that, of course. Why don't you just find yourself a female you *do* like and spend your free hours with her?"

"Not yet," George replied, abruptly.

Walker wisely did not pursue the topic. "Pretend you have one, then you can do as you please."

George thought a moment. "Thank you, sir." As nothing further seemed to be forthcoming he turned for the door.

"Have you found the man you are looking for?"

"The man?" George was startled, not realising that his constant look-out for his Uncle Samuel had been noticed. "How do you know that, captain?"

"I don't miss much, boy, and I've seen you peering aboard every ship which docks near us. Who are you seeking?"

"My uncle — Sam Mitchell."

If Walker made a mental note of the differing surname he probably imagined that Mitchell was George's maternal family name: all he said was, "I served with a Mitchell once, years ago: a fine seaman. If you don't set us all alight you might, one day, follow his good example."

★ ★ ★

In England, tied up to the quay at the Hythe, George found himself able to go ashore without fear of the Runners or a meeting with one of his family. After several months at sea he had grown a beard which altered his appearance

103

so that he was confident acquaintances would not recognise him and carry tales to Langetts. He scanned the local newsheets and could find no mention of a murder at Helmdon and allowed himself the luxury of releasing himself from the torment of the dreams which disturbed his much-needed rest.

After a year at sea he had almost forgotten the misery of living with his mother's scorn and her subsequent fall from grace. He was a sailor now and with luck and good health saw a future which promised him an eventual command of his own in fulfulment of his boyhood hopes.

6

IN the spring of 1793 the count de
la Bellefontaine was a most unhappy
man. Everything he had dreaded had
befallen the country of his birth, and he
had made up his mind that, whether his
wife wished it or not, she and Magdalena
must escape to a friendly court.

Two years earlier Louis XVI and his
family had made an abortive attempt to
run away from the Tuileries and join the
thousands of their noble compatriots who
had already been sufficiently fortunate to
find refuge in Germany or Austria. Their
flight had been hampered by an inability
to grasp that speed was essential and a
minimum of food and clothing the best
for which they might hope.

On their ignominious return to Paris
Louis had been forced to accept the new
constitution of the National Assembly
and, against his will, declare war upon
his wife's native Austria. Further shame
was thrust upon him as the Church was

declared illegal and Marie Antoinette was branded an empty-headed whore. Helplessly the king and his consort saw the dissolution of their known existence with the massacre of their personal troops, The Swiss Guard, and the sacking of their palace.

In 1792 the September Massacres had claimed the lives of priests, schoolmasters and minor gentry: no one was safe. La Bellefontaine had bitten his nails to the quick as he weighed up his own family's chances of reaching safety: with autumn approaching the early snows would already be making the mountains impassable and he was certain that there was no time to be lost; yet he hesitated, torn between two unbearable anxieties.

His worst fears were confirmed when Louis was guillotined in the following January of 1793 after standing trial for a so-called plan of counter-revolution. It was only a matter of time before the mob called for the blood of the queen and her two children.

★ ★ ★

On one particularly tranquil afternoon, warmed with early sunshine, the countess was also frightened, although it would have been difficult to detect a symptom of fear in her upright form and her unwavering gaze. The object of her terror was a letter she had received from a friend who had been a lady-in-waiting to Marie Antoinette but had been separated from the queen after the flight to Varennes. This woman wrote to the countess without sparing any detail of the anarchy which now reigned in Paris and other parts of the country.

' . . . and the Bonnets Rouges are everywhere, flaunting their ill-gotten power and shouting the rubbish that has been fed to them by evil men like Danton, Marat and Robespierre. Gentlewomen are raped in their homes and they and their menfolk are bundled into tumbrils to be thrown into filthy prisons to await 'trials' which can only end in one way — the guillotine. When you receive this letter do not hesitate to flee for your lives. Those of us who have striven to be good employers have suffered with the frivolous, and when the people about you are infected with the poison that is ruining our country you will not be spared. I never thought to live to see churches where I have worshipped and found comfort in communion with God daubed with slogans of Liberté, Egalité and Fraternité. Why! The very altars at which we have been blessed have been desecrated with pagan sacrifices and worse.

'Please give heed to my warning: I cannot urge you sufficiently strongly to depart from your home before you are compelled to witness atrocities such as will haunt me to my dying day.

'The messenger is a trusted secretary of the family in Coblentz where I have found refuge: he will, I know, advise you not to return with him but to make arrangements to travel to a small port or beach near Bordeaux where an English fisherman or trader might be persuaded to take you to England. Friends who have made the journey write to tell me they are well received despite the intelligentsia's flirtation with the early revolution — and the war which has broken out between our two countries . . . '

★ ★ ★

So that when the count finally made up his mind and came into the room to broach the subject of an early departure from the château, he found the countess in a subdued and acquiescent mood. He did not hesitate to show his delight when he heard that madame thought Magdalena should be sent from her home without delay.

"My dear, I have been worrying about this for weeks — months. I am *so* pleased that you have come to see the sense of flight at last!" He stooped to kiss his wife's cheek. "When can you be ready to leave?"

"I'm not going. Nothing would induce me to leave my home; I would rather be dead than allow that rabble to inhabit la Bellefontaine. But Magdalena, Mamselle and M. Fourré must be gone as soon as it is possible."

"But, my dear wife, you cannot remain here."

"Are you going?" She looked at him intently, and when he did not answer, she continued: "Of course not, and where you stay, I remain."

"But — "

"There are no buts: you had not really imagined I should leave?" When her husband gave her a look of despair, she went on: "That does not mean I think there is no danger. What plans or thought of a possible destination have you for our daughter and her escorts?"

"I've had a thousand ideas during many sleepless nights — the Rhine — England even."

"The latter was suggested to me in this letter brought to me today by secret courier, but I do not favour the thought of Magdalena finding sanctuary amongst our enemies. As far as the Rhine is concerned, my correspondent tells me not to consider that route as most of the countryside is imbued with the Parisian madness and German troops are on the move."

"If that is the case, what would *you* suggest?" The count was pale with anxiety at the prospect of casting the die for their daughter's future.

"I should settle, without question, on the court of Naples."

"But consider the journey through the Alps!"

"They are not insurmountable with a trusted guide, and M. Fourré can contact that young duc who came here with Bastien, he has land around Castellane."

"I don't like it; it is altogether too difficult."

"All the more reason for success."

"But Magdalena is so young and unworldly!"

"Our daughter has more to her than her looks." The countess stopped as she heard her husband sniff, and went on hurriedly, "Just think of the assets of Naples! Maria Carolina is a sister of Marie Antoinette and is known to me from my days as lady-in-waiting to the queen."

"Maria Carolina is married to the most grotesque barbarian in Christendom."

"Ferdinand?" The countess managed a twist of the lips, which might have been a smile. "Don't worry about Magdalena's virtue where he is concerned: he is more interested in boar hunting than chasing young ladies. Besides, he has a monstrous number of children, for Carolina does not fail in her marital duties however gross her husband might be."

"Well, let us consider Naples." The count moved to the bell-rope and a servant in plain livery came to answer the summons. "Please bring M. Fourré from the library to me. The count moved to the window and looked out on to the gardens where already the blossom was festooning the trees and birds swooped over the flower-beds, which showed obvious signs of neglect, in search of twigs and moss for their nests. "Before we go too far in our deliberations we must discover if our priestly friend would entertain the idea of escorting two gentlewomen on such a hazardous mission."

M. Fourré, a man of medium height and stocky build, came into the salon and bowed to the countess. "My lord?" he said.

"Sit down, man." The count's tone was more brusque than usual, and the curé seated himself without fuss on a gilt chair at a respectful distance from the countess.

"Is there something I can do for you and your family, monseigneur?"

It was the countess who answered. "M. Fourré, I have received information today which has made me come to a decision about Magdalena's future — " She hesitated, uncertain for once how to make demands upon another person. Would the priest be willing to risk his life to save that of a sheltered, pampered girl?

"You are about to ask me to escort the young countess and Mamselle away from here, are you not, madame?" The voice was calm and the dark-complexioned face expressionless.

The count, taken aback by the priest's quick understanding, stammered that this was, indeed, the very matter which he and his wife wished to discuss. "You would be willing to undertake this hazardous expedition?"

"More than that: I should be glad of an opportunity to repay some of the kindness which you and *la comtesse* have shown me since my position as parish priest became untenable."

"I cannot express my deep gratitude!" the countess exclaimed, her face colouring under the powder and paint which she still used.

"There is no need because I comprehend, only too well, the dilemma which you face. Without being a parent it is still possible to judge the feelings of a mother and father who are parting with their greatest treasure — perhaps for ever." He was quiet for a moment, and then said, very gently, "I have never forgotten the look in my mother's eyes when I broke the news that I was entering the priesthood."

"We shall be for ever in your debt." The count moved to stand at the curé's side. "Before you came in we were discussing possible destinations; my wife is of the opinion that the court of Naples offers the best hope of sanctuary."

"My own view, exactly. England is our enemy and unknown to any of us, while Flanders or the Rhineland are only reached by crossing the hostile environs of Paris."

"You seem to have given the matter some thought."

"Mamselle and I have discussed it daily, with, if I may venture to say so, growing alarm. Each day your daughter lingers at la Bellefontaine the danger to her person grows. I understand the reasons for your hesitation and hope that once we are gone you will see no reason to remain here."

"We shall stay here, whatever the menace, because someone must hold the estate in trust for Magdalena until she may return and claim her inheritance."

There was a moment of silence, then the countess asked that if Mamselle and M. Fourré had talked of helping her daughter to escape, had they any plans to put forward.

"Indeed we have," the priest exclaimed, glad to drop the distasteful topic of the stubborn refusal of the count and his wife to realise the inevitability of the holocaust which was about to shatter their existence.

"Tell us of them."

"Mamselle and I thought that if I took upon myself the guise of a pedlar we might pass muster as a family of the people going about their business."

"It seems an excellent suggestion. Would you think that a couple of mules or donkeys would be permissible for the ladies to ride?"

"We considered this matter and came to the conclusion that for a hundred miles or so from here the poverty of the Parisian outskirts is not apparent and mounts would not be as noticeable as in other regions. Donkeys would be less conspicuous than mules, they live off the land and we might be able to take three — one being ostensibly laden with my 'wares'."

"Can we find the animals?" asked the countess.

"There are several used in the fields for drawing water from the wells which could be replaced from the stables of the château," said her husband. "I can arrange to have them brought in without too much attention being drawn to the change-over."

"If that is settled there remains the question of suitable clothing."

"Mamselle has seen to it that a supply of servants' dresses have found their way to the wardrobe of *la comtesse* Magdalena and I have sufficient friends left among the peasants to find a pair of breeches and a leather jerkin."

The count glanced at the priest's

soutane and said that there would be no need to ask in the nearby village for clothes as he could furnish Fourré with some of his old hunting-gear. "The less is known about the doings in the château the less mouths there are to talk." He turned to his wife, "Shall we have the child come in so that we may speak with her?"

Madame inclined her head. "And Mamselle had better accompany her as her presence will make it less painful for us all."

Bowing, the curé went to fetch the pair from the library and, as Magdalena came into the salon, tears blurred her father's sight. She was more solemn than in the carefree days of her birthday three years earlier, but the serious air had given her beauty an added poignancy. Curls no longer fell about her shoulders, and her hair was coiled up on her head to make her look taller and more dignified. She curtsied to her mother and sat down in a chair indicated by the count. The governess and the priest stood behind her in a protective gesture.

Making a great effort at composure

the count told his daughter that she was
going to leave La Bellefontaine and seek
refuge in the court of Naples.

Magdalena looked up. "You think it is
necessary for us to find sanctuary until
the country recovers its sanity?"

"We do," the countess replied, "and
for that reason we have discussed the best
means of accomplishing your safety and
have agreed with M. Fourré that he will
escort you and Mamselle on, what might
well be, a long and dangerous journey."

"But we are all going?" Alarm leapt
into the expressive eyes.

"No." It was the countess who replied
in firm tones which plainly indicated that
no arguing would be permissible.

Nevertheless Magdalena was not to
be gainsaid. "But you and Father must
leave also; I have hoped every day since
the king's death that you would see the
wisdom of leaving our home until such
time as we may return to it in peace."

"My child," the count said, "you *must*
go, but your mother and I shall remain
in the hope that what we fear is a menace
of our imagination."

"Then I shall stay also!" The young

voice rang out in the beautiful room with its elegant furnishings. Magdalena sat very straight on her chair, her cheeks flushed and her eyes wide.

"You will leave as soon as M. Fourré and your father can bring mounts to the house and Mamselle and you have had an opportunity to try on the clothes which she has been hoarding against this day."

"I *cannot* leave here without you!" Magdalena now made no effort to stop the tears which seemed to come welling up from the tight constriction about her chest and throat.

"My child," her father replied, taking her hands and pulling her to her feet to hold her in his arms, "don't make it more difficult for us. You are young, with all your life to enjoy, your mother and I have had many contented years together. At worst we can only lose our lives, but spare us the agony of watching our beloved only child suffering at the hands of these ignoramuses who have set themselves up as our masters."

"But I may never see you again!"

"Yes; that is possible, but give us, at

least, the comfort of knowing that there is a chance you will be spared to give us grandchildren."

"Of what use would they be without you to enjoy them?"

The countess spoke sharply. "Let there be an end to this argument! We lose valuable time while we discuss a hypothetical future. Mamselle, be so good as to take our child to her apartments and help her to become accustomed to wearing the dress of a pedlar's daughter."

"Mama!" The cry was distraught.

"Go, my child, and think yourself fortunate that you have good friends who are willing to risk their lives in an effort to save yours."

Magdalena went from the salon, her shoulders drooping and her feet dragging on the marble floor. When the doors closed behind her, her mother rose hurriedly and went to the window where she made no attempt to stop the flow of tears which coursed down her cheeks, sadly marring the porcelain artistry of her complexion.

Helplessly the count and the priest set

about the business of finding donkeys, food, and wares to sell.

★ ★ ★

In her bedroom Magdalena allowed herself to be helped out of her silk dress and fine linen shift and stays and put on a coarse cotton petticoat and overdress of kersey. Almost without realising what she was doing she took off her delicate silk stockings, which were decorated with fancy clocks of embroidered roses, and donned thick woollen hose. With difficulty she forced her feet into a pair of flat, latchet shoes which had been made in the village for a girl no longer in the service of the household.

"Now your hair," Mamselle said crisply, without meeting her charge's eye.

Mechanically Magdalena sat down on the stool at her dressing-table and took out the pins which held the shining braids about her head. Mamselle made no effort to assist her, for, although the girl had had no personal maid during the past months, Mamselle had sometimes helped in the elaborate toilette. Now was the moment to underline the necessity that Magdalena must henceforth care for her own appearance. "Brush it well."

Magdalena picked up the silver-backed brush and watched, in silence, as her hair fell about her shoulders and touched her waist. Turning her head she said without expression, "It will have to be cut a little for it will be difficult to manage as it is."

Mamselle gave an inward sigh of relief at this first sign of co-operation and brought scissors to cut the abundant tresses to shoulder length. "Don't worry, my dear, once at the court of Naples you will be free to let it fall to your knees, if you so wish."

"Naples! I would prefer a thousand times to stay here."

"Try to be sensible and understand your parents have good reasons for sending you away."

"I don't want to go."

"Have you learnt nothing from your years of study?" Mamselle's voice was sharp with anxiety and exasperation.

"You have read so much from the works recommended to you that I would have thought you had understood the rationale of accepting good advice."

Magdalena sighed. "Forgive me, Mamselle, I have suffered a shock which has robbed me of my power to reason." She straightened her shoulders and regarded her reflection in the looking-glass. "Will I pass muster?"

"Beauty is not the prerogative of the rich," her companion remarked mildly, "and with your hands rubbed in some good garden soil you could well be the daughter of a travelling packman." Mamselle wished that her inward convictions were as sound as her outward expression.

"How shall we go to Naples?"

"By following the Loire, then south to the Alps and beyond to the sea where we hope to find a ship."

"The Alps?" A little colour came in the girl's pale cheeks. "Does that mean that we shall go near Castellane?"

"Almost certainly, for M. Fourré and I have talked of many routes and abandoned all in favour of the one through the Alpes Basses towards Cisteron. It is an unlikely way for escaping aristos to take in view of its difficulties — most would choose the road towards Avignon and the coast."

"Then, if we go to Castellane we have at least a friend at hand."

"The duc de Baron?"

"You remember him?"

"Yes," Mamselle replied drily, for it would have been difficult to have forgotten the fair-haired, soberly dressed young man who had changed her pupil from a carefree child to a thoughtful and gifted young woman. "Now I think it is time for me to find some suitable clothing while you look in the bundle for another pair of stockings and shoes, a cloak and a petticoat."

"Will that be sufficient for a long journey?"

"It would constitute the entire wardrobe of a young woman in the station which you will now enjoy, and I suggest you make yourself proficient at dressing in the strange clothing and then find yourself a shawl to use as a bundle for a brush, a comb and few necessities."

"No jewellery of course," Magdalena said, while she went about the business of selecting the items Mamselle had mentioned.

"No jewellery as you rightly suggest, but a linen cap or two and a woollen bonnet to keep out the cold."

★ ★ ★

Unexpectedly a little of the misery ebbed and was replaced by a sense of adventure, not unconnected with the thought of that unusual young man who had haunted her dreams. Would they reach Castellane in safety, and would François remember her?

Bastien had not been to her home in months, and since the revolution letters were not delivered unless by trusted messengers. She had had no word from François for nearly two years; it was most likely he had other things to think of than the heiress of la Bellefontaine.

7

MAGDALENA, Mamselle and Fourré left la Bellefontaine two days later — two days spent in making urgent and secret preparation for their departure. The count was a liberal-minded and just landowner, but it was impossible to judge how many of the outrageous ideas of the new men of France had been brought to the pleasant, fruitful countryside of the Loire; no one could be trusted absolutely.

Fourré bought two donkeys from a couple of farmers who had good reason to look upon his requests for favours without asking too many questions, and these were brought to the château stable where the grooms were led to believe that the young countess was disposing of her Arabian fillies to replace them with more plebeian mounts. Fourré also found stout panniers, and with the help of the count decided he would specialise in selling haberdashery: these articles being the most easily come by in the château. "Mind now," the countess warned her daughter and Mamselle as they sorted through piles of ribbons, laces and trimmings, "nothing too ornate, for you are catering for the bourgeoisie."

The older woman noted with a pang that her child seemed almost to enjoy the task and envied her the youthful zest which made a perilous journey into a near-holiday. Yet she would not have it otherwise, for it would have broken her heart to see Magdalena pining too much or afraid of the difficulties which lay ahead. The countess was well aware that her daughter could have no real conception of what dangers she might face but she knew, also, that Magdalena was intelligent enough to be realistic.

Under Mamselle's tuition the girl made a belt of soft kid like that of her own to tie about her waist, into the pockets of which went sufficient gold Louis' to see them through the months of travel ahead. Fourré also stowed away jewels among his bobbins of silk and stores of pins and needles.

In the privacy of her own rooms

Magdalena practised putting on and taking off the simple garments which had at first filled her with disgust. As she donned them in the dark hour before the dawn in which they were to slip away from her home, she remarked to Mamselle that she was coming to believe the peasants had an enviable lot in dressing as they did, for their simple garments were far easier to wear than the elaborate and often uncomfortable stiff silks and whalebone to which she was accustomed.

"And what a pleasure it is not to have to dress my hair!" she exclaimed, pulling on a round, knitted cap.

"I don't think the girls who have never had a prettier dress than the one you are now wearing would agree with you, but there is much to be said for garments less demanding than those called for at court or in your life here."

Magdalena stood up from her dressing-stool and walked slowly round her ornate bedchamber, touching a hanging or a piece of well-polished furniture. Mamselle thought it was almost as if the girl was saying goodbye to the possessions which

128

had surrounded her since birth, but was surprised when Magdalena said: "Do you think I can carry off the rôle of being yours and M. Fourré's daughter?"

"Of course you can!"

"But I have led such a sheltered and spoilt existence here."

"You have learnt a great deal of late, and your common sense will stand you in good stead. Come now," Mamselle said, thinking that this was the appropriate moment to inject a little acerbity into the proceedings, "pick up your bundle and tie your cloak about you: we must find your papa and mama and make our farewells."

Magdalena did as she was told, and without a backward glance followed her governess to her mother's boudoir. At the sight of the countess in a pale grey peignoir covered with delicate Valenciennes lace it was almost more than she could do to stop herself bursting into tears, but she had resolved during a sleepless night that she would put on as bold a face as possible before her parents and, if she must cry, indulge her emotions once she was safely away from the château. Her mother had obviously made similar resolutions and contented herself with last-minute pleas for the greatest care of their tongues and behaviour. "Do not forget that from now on you were born at Sancerre, in the house at the top of the hill next to the wine-growers, and that M. Fourré, your father, has always travelled the countryside (which is true) following his trade, and goes now to Nevers to visit his ailing mother. Once you are passed Nevers the same story will serve for the next large town you will reach, and so on: and, I implore you, do not *ever* be led into talking to the most trustworthy-seeming confidant about your true identity. Remember, nothing said has never to be regretted. I wish, my child, that I could put about your neck the pearls I had been keeping for your wedding day but will content myself with giving you my love and prayers instead."

"But I shall be here for my wedding!"

"I hope so." The countess' voice was strangely even. "Now take leave of your father."

Magdalena took one look at the count's

face and was about to announce that nothing but brute force would remove her from la Bellefontaine when she felt Mamselle gently push her towards her father who seemed, suddenly, old and helpless. She knelt for his blessing and, from a long way off, heard him whisper his farewells and God speed.

Supported by M. Fourré and Mamselle she went out of the room, and by means of the cold, stone staircase behind the panelling of the boudoir came eventually to cavernous cellars into which she had never been before. In a daze which bordered on the nightmare of her childhood, she allowed herself to be guided to the stables where M. Fourré helped her mount one of the donkeys and, after assisting Mamselle to the back of another, held up a lantern and led them as noiselessly as possible across the cobbled yard to the gates of the mews. From the trees by the river an owl hooted and a cat, frightened by the muffled hooves of the donkeys, fled squawking into the gardens.

Magdalena held her breath expecting the hounds, which her father kept for hunting, to bark furiously, but they were obviously used to the nocturnal habits of their feline friends and ignored them.

The gates opened noiselessly, and Magdalena guessed M. Fourré had seen to it that the hinges were well oiled. She had always admired his academic skills but had been surprised during the last two days of intense preparation by his grasp of practical matters. When she had remarked on this, Mamselle had told her that Fourré came from farming stock and had had great difficulty in convincing his family that he felt the call of caring for souls rather than animals and crops.

It was easier going once the orchards were reached, and they turned to take a last look at the château where a single window was illumined by a branch of candles. Magdalena waved her farewells, knowing that her gesture was futile and that it would be impossible for her parents to catch a glimpse of the little party as it left the shelter of the grounds. Now the tears she had been holding back would no longer be gainsaid, and she sobbed quietly and helplessly into the folds of her hooded cloak.

The small track towards Sancerre was well known, and the donkeys quietly picked their way through the ruts to pass through the sleeping hamlet of Lerc. As they neared the forest of Charmes a pale light crept into the eastern sky and showed them the still waters of the canal du Loire at their left.

"Let us break our fasts here," Fourré said, "so that we may make as much progress as possible in daylight to la Charité: it is my intention not to shun small villages and towns (where my goods may be welcomed) but to avoid cities where the extremists of the Revolution are constantly on guard for Girondish sympathisers and the likes of us."

"But we have our passes," Magdalena exclaimed.

"Indeed we have but I doubt they would stand up to the scrutiny of an educated Jacobin."

Mamselle laughed. "You are casting doubts upon my skill at forgery, *mon padre*."

"Take care," Fourré said quickly, "you must remember that I am now Hubert and you are Emilia."

"Forgive me," Mamselle sighed, "I forgot; it is so difficult after all these years to think of you other than as our confessor."

"Well, *ma mère*," Magdalena put in, "imagine how difficult it will be for me to have two sets of parents — and how fortunate," she added.

The sun was climbing above the low hills to the east as they sighted Sancerre standing on the hill above their route, and they were met by drovers with their cattle and farm workers carrying bill-hooks or yokes with half-empty pails of milk. Apart from a mumbled greeting their appearance seemed to arouse little curiosity. Once or twice as they ambled alongside the canal Magdalena saw Fourré glance over his shoulder. The apprehension which was constantly with her made her heart beat a little faster but, almost as if the priest recognised her anxiety, he looked back no more, and they rode on in silence until Fourré suggested they ate their midday meal in a small wood they could see ahead.

"We should be in St. Bouize soon after we have eaten and should reach la

134

Charité in time to find a bed and such food as is available."

"Shall we try to sell some of our wares in St. Bouize?" Magdalena asked.

"I think we should not waste time today but may well take the opportunity of establishing ourselves as itinerant merchants when we find an inn tonight." He excused himself and wandered off into the trees and dead bracken.

Relaxing beneath the budding branches and listening to the birds sing as they flitted in and out of the sunshine Magdalena saw the Loire glinting in the distance. Never far from her thoughts the memory of the taut little scene in her mother's boudoir returned to her with a sadness which caught at her throat. Abruptly she held out her pewter mug for another helping of wine and drank it quickly; it was impossible not to brood upon the security of her home-life, but that was, temporarily, behind her and she must concentrate all her efforts on keeping faith with her parents and fulfilling their wishes for her safety.

"Eat this, my child," Mamselle said, offering a piece of cold pie, "this food might well be the last easily obtained meal we shall see."

Magdalena ate in silence, surprised that she was hungry, and then said, looking about her, "*Mon père* seems to have been gone a long time."

"Indeed he has. I thought he had but gone to answer a call of nature. Perhaps he has found something to interest him in the woods; I know he is a keen ornithologist."

"But surely he would not be watching birds when he was, only a short time ago, urging that we must put as much ground between us and la Bellefontaine as possible."

"That's true, so what can have become of him?"

Magdalena stood up, shaking off the crumbs which clung to her fustian skirt, and ventured to the edge of the wood. A long way off she saw the stout figure of the priest walking towards her on the track they had been following. She returned to Mamselle. "*Ma mère*, it is very strange, but he approaches from Sancerre."

Mamselle looked up, puzzled. "What

could have made him return that way?"

Magdalena shrugged. "I did see him looking back over his shoulders once or twice and wondered what he was about."

Neither women spoke until Fourré came to where they waited beneath the trees. His face was red and running with sweat, Magdalena passed him bread and wine while Mamselle probed: "What *have* you been doing?"

Fourré drank deeply. "Some instinct told me we were being followed."

"No!" both women exclaimed in dismay.

"When we stopped I went back through the trees past the bend which hides the road from here and found a man walking purposefully, but somewhat nervously, towards us. I hid behind the bole of an oak until he was almost level and then walked out, as casually as possible, to confront him. You can imagine my astonishment when I recognised one of the grooms from the château."

"A groom?" Magdalena echoed. "Then we are, perhaps, lost before we have gone a day's journey."

"That was my reasoning, but I questioned the man exhaustively until I'm nearly convinced that he is in earnest when he says that he wishes only to help us."

"But how can we be absolutely certain he means us no harm? It seems a strange thing to be following us at a distance like this." Mamselle's voice was edged with anxiety. "Yet surely, if he meant to make us known to the local representative of the Jacobins he had but to walk into Sancerre and we should, by now, be in the hands of the Revolutionaries."

"Exactly my reasoning," Fourré said.

"Who is he?" Magdalena asked.

"He says his name is Pierre Lebrun."

"Lebrun! Ah, my worst fears are somewhat put at rest to hear that name, for Lebrun taught me to ride and has always been kind and helpful. Is he a tall man with a pockmarked face?"

"He is."

"What does he want?" Mamselle asked. "Have you sent him back?"

"He says he wants to act as a bodyguard to the little countess — to our daughter — for he admits to an

138

admiration for Magdalena which he has carried in his heart since she first sat a pony. Would you say, Magdalena, that Lebrun ever gave you cause to suspect he admired you?"

"Admired me? But he is an old man — quite thirty-five years old if he is a day?"

Mamselle and Fourré laughed ruefully. "Not much of an age, really. *Did* you have occasion to believe he was fond of you?"

"No, of course not! Lebrun was always respectful and — and attentive. What have you done with him?"

"I've allowed him to follow us at a distance as it seemed impossible to do anything else. He protested his complete loyalty to the house of la Bellefontaine and offered to hand me his papers as surety."

"Has he food and clothing?" Mamselle enquired with an eye to the practicability of an extra mouth to feed.

"He confesses that he only grabbed a hunk of bread and a flask of wine when he made up his mind to follow us."

"Then we did awake someone when

we left the stables!" Magdalena cried.

"Apparently we did. Lebrun confesses to have been on watch and to have dozed off only to be awoken by a screeching cat."

"Well," Mamselle said slowly, "I'm not sure that I am entirely happy with this turn of events, but can only say that he could be a help to us and pray that our faith in him is not falsely lodged."

"Time alone will show, and if he does not dog our footsteps too closely and we have any reason to doubt him, we shall have to find ways and means of doubling back on our tracks and losing him. I think it best to meet him now and then leave him to rest while we push on for la Charité."

Magdalena was never to forget the mixture of misgiving and pleasure which she experienced when she saw Pierre Lebrun. When he attempted to kneel to her she hastily gestured for him to rise and told him that she was now *citoyenne* Magdalena Flavert and that the curé and her governess were now her 'parents'.

It was possible that his unconscious act of homage did more than his protestations to Fourré, and instinct told her that what she read in his eyes was not an affected emotion but a genuine desire to be of service.

When he refused some of the meagre remains of the smuggled food he went up in Mamselle's estimation. "I don't want to be a burden so I shall fend for myself."

"But what will you do for money?" Fourré asked. "Food is fairly plentiful here, but I imagine that in the districts bordering Lyon and other Jacobin centres the citizens will not have sufficient to feed themselves, let alone a beggar."

"I'll earn my keep, never fear, and will be on hand should occasion arise."

Fourré had finished eating by now, and he helped his 'wife' and 'daughter' to the saddles of their donkeys. "We shall be on our way, *citoyen*."

They came to la Charité at dusk, mingling with the inhabitants as they returned from their daily toil. Fourré selected the smaller of the two inns, and the party rode in under the arched doorway into a small, galleried yard.

Magdalena found her heart was racing

as she slid down with unfeigned weariness to the cobbles: it was one thing to ride her sleek thoroughbreds on their morning gallops but quite another to sit on a small and uncomfortable saddle for most of the day. Especially a day that was fraught with loss and the omnipresent fear of being discovered.

Fourré, assuming the broad accents of his native Provence, sought out the host of the inn and found there was shelter available in communal rooms for himself and the two women. "They don't seem too particular in the niceties of life," he muttered as he unhooked his pedlar's baskets, "and they say I may bring in my wares but I mustn't expect to sell anything for money is short."

"Someone may be tempted," Mamselle said as she led her mount to the stable and motioned Magdalena to do the same. "Don't stand there gaping, girl; if you want some supper see to it the donkey has his first."

Magdalena stifled a gasp of surprise and, in a valiant attempt to ape the behaviour of a daughter of the people, shrugged her shoulders and lugged the exhausted beast into the low shed which served as a stable.

The inn was full of people, young soldiers on their way to join their regiments on the north and eastern fronts, and villagers exchanging the gossip of the day. Fourré led his party to the darkest corner of the beamed room and asked for bowls of soup. When it came it proved surprisingly good, and Magdalena could have eaten more but Mamselle stood up and she could do nothing but follow her adopted parent up the ladder to the loft above. She was so tired that she noticed neither the rank straw, the stale air, nor the bugs which attacked her delicate skin.

In the morning Fourré roused them early, and aching in every limb Magdalena smoothed out her dress, made an effort to comb out the tangles of her hair and went down to the inn parlour. Her appearance was greeted with whistles by the young soldiers who were about to depart, but Mamselle ignored their overtures, and the three of them ate hunks of bread washed down with thin beer.

"No customers here," Fourré growled. "We'd best be on our way or 'my mother' will be dead before we reach her."

He paid the reckoning with a coin he searched for in his leather breeches and joined the women who were already mounted on the donkeys. Amazed he asked, "Surely you have not done all this so quickly? How did you lift the baskets and secure them."

Magdalena replied, her voice expressionless, "A fellow traveller was good enough to feed and water the beasts and assisted us while you were paying the innkeeper."

Fourré raised his eyebrows. "Where is the man?"

"Gone," Mamselle supplied.

"Then let us be on our way."

Magdalena dug her heels into the sides of her donkey and followed Fourré as he led Mamselle and her panniered mount out into the main street of the town. Silently they passed in front of a magnificent basilica where the barred doors told of its abuse and headed for the wide bridge which connected the two halves of the ancient township.

Magdalena saw rotting barges tied to the wharves of what had once been an important port and heard Fourré say that it was a pity the broad, fast-flowing river, with its many sandy islands, was no longer a viable means of transport. "We'd make much better time in a boat than on these poor beasts," he said, "as we should if we could use the canal in safety."

"We seem to have passed our first hurdle with no mishap," Mamselle volunteered.

"Oh, *maman*," Magdalena cried, "don't tempt the fates, we have so many towns to confront before we reach our destination."

8

FROM the town the countryside was open, rolling up to the foothills of the Côte du Nivernais. Peasants, men and women, hoed the fields flanking the road, and some called out greetings to the travellers. Near Argonviers Fourré sold his first piece of goods, a length of ribbon to a girl who confessed she was hoping to be married in the summer.

Fourré pocketed the small coin, and Magdalena saw that he involuntarily began to make the sign of benediction but recovered himself in time to point to some hawks wheeling in the sky above them.

The priest had filled their food-basket with a flagon of wine and some sour bread and cheese. This they ate before recrossing the Loire to enter the walled town of Nevers.

Magdalena drank a fair share of the sharp wine and was glad of the courage it gave her, for it was at the gate of the town that a shabbily dressed soldier of the Republic asked for their papers. While these were being inspected Magdalena demurely fluttered her eyelids at his companion who lounged against the wall of the gatehouse. This worthy made bold enough to exchange banter with Mamselle about the baggage they sold being no better than the baggage they brought with them, and Mamselle answered him back with an acid retort which seemed to please the fellow. Magdalena found herself, once more, amazed at the prowess of her late governess in assuming the very character of the woman she feigned to be. Not trusting herself to speak Magdalena made mental notes for use on future occasions, and heard, with great relief, the sergeant (or so his stripes proclaimed) giving surly permission for them to proceed into the old city.

Here in front of the cathedral a market of sorts was in progress, and Fourré told them he intended to set up his wares for a short time so that the women could buy food and he could listen to the chatter of the passers-by.

It was while Mamselle was making a purchase of some brawn that Magdalena caught sight of Lebrun standing some way off in the shade of a budding plane-tree. He gave no sign of recognition although he stared straight towards her, and the girl found this disconcerting but, at the same time, strangely reassuring. Magdalena had heard many tales of trusted servants suddenly turning on their one-time masters, but Lebrun's actions to date gave no indication of treachery, and his help in saddling the donkeys and securing the heavy panniers had been invaluable.

Food was not plentiful in the few stalls which sold produce, but Mamselle bought coarse pâté, more wine and some wizened apples which had obviously lain in store since the autumn. Fourré exchanged a length of tape and a few pins for a pot of curd cheese and then moved to another pitch at the opposite side of the square where he remained for half an hour or so. Magdalena had seen a stall full of pretty pottery as they picked their way through the trestles, and she begged Fourré to barter for three plates which they might use and sell at a later date. Fourré left the women to sell their wares, and with the look of a father who is used to giving his child her every want exchanged a length of cotton (which had once been a dust-sheet at the château) for the coveted platters.

"You are so kind, *mon père*," Magdalena smiled. "Our food will taste much nicer from now on."

"Well, don't be setting your heart on the speciality of every town," Mamselle said crisply, "or we shall end up with iron-ware, glass and heavens knows what else."

Contrite Magdalena said she would remember and, stowing the plates in the food-basket which was her responsibility, climbed to the saddle as Fourré gave the word to move off.

They spent the next week travelling at a good rate but without any undue haste which might have called attention to themselves. They stayed in inns of varying degrees of cleanliness at Décize, Gamot, Doupière and Digion.

Afterwards they were to recall this gentle breaking-in to a new life as a quiet period which, in retrospect, was almost pleasant.

★ ★ ★

Fourré gave much thought to the matter of passing through Lyon. Lyon was known to be loyal to the monarchy, but with the rise of the Jacobin movement and the growing resistance to the moderates there was a constant threat to the ancient city which might, at any moment, erupt into a siege situation. It would be highly dangerous to be among friends but cut off from all escape routes.

The priest decided to take the southern route through Roanne and the range of mountains known as des Mollières to the ancient town of Vienne on the Rhône.

They travelled now more and more slowly as they climbed to the Col de Malval and descended into the valley to ascend yet again the hilly country about Mornat.

Here Fourré was delighted to discover a Roman aqueduct, but Magdalena had other things to concern her than the antiquities of a past civilisation. For herself she had never felt better, the constant exercise, the diet of plain fare and the new aspect of France enlivening her and helping her to forget the reason for her journey.

With Mamselle it was otherwise; born a gentlewoman and reared in an atmosphere of refinement and education, she lacked the resilience which is inherent to the aristocrat who is close to the soil. Magdalena noticed that Mamselle fretted over her inability to wash herself properly and viewed with distaste the alarming manner in which their clothing became daily more soiled and travel-worn. It was not that the older woman grumbled or expressed a word of complaint: she was, in fact, in constant vigilance for Magdalena's safety and comfort, but the girl knew that she slept badly on the dirty straw palliasses they shared and ate less and less of the unpalatable food they were able to obtain.

Wending their way slowly alongside the fast-flowing Rhône towards Vienne, Magdalena spoke of her worries to Fourré. "*Mon père*, have you not noticed that *ma mère* appears to be in some danger of falling ill?"

"Ill?" Fourré echoed, startled. "Why no, I've been more taken up with pushing and pulling these reluctant little beasts over these dratted hills to have given more than a passing thought to the poor woman."

"Do you think it would be possible to find some presentable inn in the town where we might rest for a day or two? We could, perhaps, wash our clothing and find sufficient hot water to bath in. It would make a pleasant change from the pump in the yard."

Fourré hesitated. "Delay might be disastrous, but it would be equally foolish to push on with a sick woman on our hands. And with Lebrun still dogging our footsteps I am never completely at ease."

"But, surely, by this time you have come to accept that Lebrun means us nothing but good! Think of the number of times he has appeared from nowhere to help us with the donkeys or one of those wretched panniers when they have slipped off the beasts' back."

"I cannot imagine why he stays so

obstinately with us."

"Could it not be because, like you, he is loyal to the house of la Bellefontaine?"

"It could be, yet I still fear he has other motives."

Magdalena looked at him for a moment. "You imagine he might have designs on my person?"

Fourré was startled into a quick disclaimer.

Magdalena smiled wryly. "I don't think you need worry, *mon père*. He would not make very much progress, and I am, no longer, the sheltered, spoilt darling that left the château nearly a month ago."

This was very true, and Fourré and Mamselle very often discussed the change which had come about in their adopted daughter. The sun, the wind and the rain had turned the delicate porcelain complexion into a golden glow of health, which only served to heighten the beauty of the bone structure and the tender curve of the wide and generous mouth. With the inhibitions of the château left behind Magdalena blossomed into a resourceful girl, who used her wits and her new-found sense of adventure to make light of inconveniences which she would have found totally unacceptable so short a time ago.

Fourré could not remember when they had eaten a proper meal of roast meat or venison, or tasted any wine but that of the local vineyard, yet Magdalena seemed to thrive on the diet. Was it not so with Mamselle? Making some excuse to the girl he went to take the leading rein of the governess' donkey, and choosing his moment looked into the woman's face. He saw, with a pang of alarm, that her complexion was ashen, her eyes sunken and her mouth held in a taut line which speaks of pain borne without complaint. He remarked on the swiftness of the current and the hopes he had of visiting the amphitheatre in the town ahead, and then asked quietly if Mamselle would care to rest a day or so if a suitable inn might be found.

He was rewarded with a sharp intake of breath followed by a rush of gratitude. "Oh, Hubert, it would be so very good to get down from the back of this horrible little beast and just lie in peace and quiet for one night at least. Is there no hospice where we might find shelter?"

"That is quite out of the question! There are no more houses of God, but there must be an inn which is better than those we have endured so far." He thought a moment. "Would you and Magdalena feel able to set up the wares in the Place while I take a look about the streets?"

"Of course." Mamselle turned her head and Magdalena rode up beside her. "We are able to make a showing of setting out the goods, are we not?"

"Most certainly!"

"Then that is settled," Fourré said. "Once we have crossed the ferry I'll seek out the most respectable hostelry and return for you in under an hour."

Although it was evening when they came at last into the town the day was still quite warm and the streets were full of townsfolk and soldiers. Tethering the beasts to the branches of a plane-tree and feeding them the grass they had gathered from the roadside, the women threw a length of cloth over one of the panniers to serve as a counter and began the business of displaying the ribbons, tapes and bobbins. These were very different now from the ones which they had originally brought with them from the château, their quality less exotic and, therefore, less likely to arouse suspicion. Fourré had made a point of buying goods wherever possible and bartering the lace of la Bellefontaine for food and shelter.

Quite soon a knot of women, mostly country-folk and bearing no resemblance to the desperadoes Magdalena had quickly learnt to pick out from the crowds, gathered around, and for a few sous or a handful of cherries bought a couple of buttons and a length of brightly coloured ribbons.

It was Magdalena who first noticed that their customers were being joined by some of the ill-kempt soldiery who lounged up and down the narrow streets leading on to the Place in front of the mutilated Cathedral of St. Paul. She took a deep breath and adopted the thickened accent of the Sancerre peasantry. She was engaged in measuring out a length of bodice-lace for a middle-aged crone when she felt a hand come round her waist and seek the curve of her breast. With admirable calm she rounded on her tormentor and raised her hand to deal his unshaven cheek a stinging blow, instead she found herself caught in an embrace which threatened to knock her backwards across the makeshift stall. Instincts of self-preservation made her fight back with a violence which surprised her. She had a glimpse of Mamselle's look of white horror, the faces of the peasant women caught between enjoyment and distaste and a ring of soldiers encouraging their colleague. It was their laughter and the sour smell of her attacker's breath which caused her to twist so that she was momentarily free of his hateful grasp. In that instance, she heard Lebrun's voice calmly asking what the devil the young soldiers thought they were about molesting his wife and aged mother-in-law.

Gratefully Magdalena allowed her one-time groom to pull her into the safety of his arms and watched in amazement as he pulled out a flint lock from his belt. "Now, get you gone, the lot of you," he growled, "and find someone more to your own taste than my woman."

"There's no marriage in these days!" one soldier boldly volunteered, although edging away as he did so.

"There's marriage where my pistol's concerned and it'll be a union between my shot and your head if you don't clear off."

In an amazingly short time the crowd drifted away, and Lebrun helped the women reload and fasten the panniers on the backs of the donkeys.

"How can we thank you?" Magdalena asked.

"I ask no gratitude but the opportunity of serving the daughter of a good master."

"But you had no business saying you were the husband of the — Magdalena," Mamselle put in, more colour in her cheeks than she had had in an age.

"I shall take no advantage, fear not, *ma belle-mère*," Pierre said with a short laugh.

Fourré came, half running, from a street leading away from the Place towards the hill at the side of the town. "What's this?" he asked, obviously concerned at seeing Lebrun with the women.

"Lebrun saved me from an over-amorous soldier," Magdalena said, her eyes modestly lowered to hide a secret smile. It had been quite a pleasurable moment to find a ready champion at her side.

"Well, well, we are grateful," Fourré conceded with reluctance. "Now we must part company for I think I've found some suitable lodgings for the ladies."

"Pierre must come with us," Magdalena cried. "He has proved himself a very useful bodyguard."

Fourré raised his eyebrows, took a look at Mamselle's face, which had now reverted to its original pallor, and agreed. His relief when Pierre took up a lowly station behind his little cavalcade was obvious, and he led them off to a small alleyway, almost hidden by the crumbling arch which bridged it. About half-way down the stone-covered path he stopped and knocked three times on an ancient, heavily studded door. Immediately this was opened and an aesthetic man and woman with simple clothing but the high cheek-bones of the born aristocrat welcomed them, barring and locking the thick door behind them. A long, dark corridor led to a square courtyard, and an outside staircase to a gallery from which bougainvillaea fell in purple cascades. Magdalena exclaimed in surprise. "But how beautiful." While Mamselle sighed with relief. "I can rest here." She allowed herself to be led away up the steps to a sheltered chamber.

A young girl appeared, wiping her hands on a coarse apron, and took Magdalena to another chamber next to that of Mamselle. Magdalena could hardly believe the cleanliness and the privacy. "You mean, this room is for me alone?"

"Yes," the girl replied, "and I'll soon bring you some hot water, towels and will wash any clothing you would like to have cleaned."

"That is all you see here," Magdalena answered, "and a very soiled petticoat and shift."

"I'll lend you a night-robe while they are being washed."

"Tell me," Magdalena said, slowly, "how is it that we come to this haven of peace and find people ready and willing to help us — 'til now we have slept on nothing but filthy straw, eaten poor food and kept a constant guard on our tongues."

"You have M. le curé to thank," the girl said. "He made discreet enquiries when he came to the town and he came here because he knew you were safer here than in the bowels of the earth or beneath the obelisk of Pilate's tomb down by the river."

"But why is that?"

"Because, mamselle, we care for the lepers of the town and no one approaches our door."

"A leper house!" Fear sprang into Magdalena's eyes and she involuntarily backed away from the spotless bed and the whitewashed walls.

"Don't be afraid, lady, we think the disease is not as easily carried as is commonly believed, nor do we think that it can be caught by accident."

"Where in God's name do you come by such outlandish ideas? Why, everyone

161

knows that lepers have to live separately and carry bells with them to warn passers-by of their approach! They are not even allowed into churches!"

"Who is — these days, milady?"

"But are you not afraid?"

"I was a little at first, but as my nunnery was closed by the order of the revolutionary guard and I was lucky to escape with my life, I determined to make recompense to God for His mercy and He led me here to this physician."

"The tall, handsome old man?"

"Yes, he, also, was a religious — an apothecary in a monastery near Marseilles, and in the course of seeking safety he stumbled upon this lazar-house and has made it his life-work to bring comfort and a prospect of relief to the sufferers. He experiments with herbs and potions and hopes that one day he will find a cure."

"But he is a saint!"

"Indeed," the girl agreed.

"And beside his charity to the afflicted, he aids fleeing aristos?"

"Yes," the girl's voice was even, "he believes that all men — all women — are

162

equal in the sight of God, and he will save you — if he is able — from a persecution he does not believe you deserve. M. Fourré told us plainly that your father was a liberal-minded man and that his daughter was of the same persuasion."

"I led a very sheltered existence before setting out on this journey."

"It would not appear so now. If you will forgive me, mamselle, your beauty is undeniable, but you have quickly taken upon yourself the rôle of a haberdasher's daughter."

"What can we do to recompense our benefactor?"

"We need money for food and dressings for our sufferers' sores."

"And the physician takes what we can give in return for sanctuary?"

"Exactly."

"It would seem very poor payment for such 'relief'."

"You would be surprised, milady, but there are those who prefer to run the gauntlet of being caught by the guard than court the risk of being affected." The girl, her face serene beneath a white starched cap, glanced round the spotless chamber. "You have no need to be afraid, we house our unfortunates in a separate part of the establishment. Now you must excuse me while I bring you water and fresh linen."

Magdalena revelled in the luxury of washing herself completely, and put on the shift which the girl brought her. Her own clothes were removed, and a bowl of excellent soup and a platter of cheese and new bread brought to her. When she had eaten she went to see how Mamselle fared and found, to her dismay, that her governess was prostrate on the narrow bed with the woman, who had greeted them, sitting at her side.

"What ails her?" Magdalena asked.

"She has a fever — perhaps an ague caught during the travels from your homeland."

Magdalena rushed to kneel at Mamselle's side. "Is she in any danger?"

"With care and a long rest she might recover, but her chances of surviving a month more of the life you have been leading are negligible."

"But what are we to do? We cannot

give her proper attention."

"You can leave her here — we are used to caring for the sick." The woman's voice was calm, detached.

"But I shall be desolate without her; she has been my companion for so many years."

"You do not wish her to die for you, do you?"

"Of course not!" Magdalena cried.

"Well, then you will have to spend your days of respite here in tending your friend and adjusting yourself to the prospect of continuing without her; after all, you have M. le curé and the other man to look after you."

"Oh, I do not care about myself. I wish we had never left home and had stayed to see out the troubles with Maman and *mon père*."

"That is a foolish wish, and one you would not allow yourself to dwell upon if you had witnessed, as I have, some of the atrocities that have been perpetuated upon young innocents such as yourself." The woman was silent for a moment. "My advice is to you to make the most of the tenuous sanctuary we are able to offer you and prepare yourself for the rigours of what lies ahead. From what I hear, you are going to need your young strength and quick-wittedness to cross the Alps and reach safety."

Magdalena looked up at the other woman. "Forgive me. I spoke out of the anguish I feel for Mamselle; if you will permit me I'll sit with her now and see to her wants; you must have many other calls upon your time."

9

IN the event Mamselle did not remain in the leper-house. When the proposal was made to her that she should be nursed to full recovery she flatly refused to fall in with the suggestion.

"But, Mamselle," Magdalena begged, "think of the dangers that lie ahead!"

"I think of nothing but the promise made to your father and mother: my health was somewhat impaired, but it is now completely recovered."

"You may think so," the elderly nun put in quietly, "but once you return to the travail and troubles of the nomadic life you may discover otherwise."

"Please listen," Magdalena asked, stroking the frail, blue-veined hand as it lay on the arm of the chair in Mamselle's room.

Mamselle shook her head. "I leave when you do."

The nun lifted her shoulders in a hopeless gesture. "You must do what you will; I only ask that you remain here a day or two longer so that you regain your maximum strength."

Mamselle looked at Magdalena. "What does M. Fourré say about our departure?"

"He is anxious to be on our way but will stay here as long as our good friends think you need."

So they took their farewells on a brilliant May morning almost a week later. Magdalena took several pieces of the gold Louis' from the belt about her waist and thanked the priest and the two nuns for the retreat and calm they had enjoyed. "We shall never forget your kindness and will think of your good works constantly."

"And we shall pray for you, little *comtesse*, and hope that you will come in safety to Naples."

They went alone down the dark passage to the side street, and Lebrun went first to ensure that the alley was empty.

"The town seems strangely deserted," M. Fourré remarked as he led Mamselle's donkey out into the main thoroughfare towards the Place.

"But I can hear much noise," Magdalena

said, as she heard shouts and excited cheering ahead.

"We had best avoid the Place and take the track across the hill," Fourré commented.

"I'll go on and see what is the matter." Lebrun slipped away, and the donkeys plodded on the steep track at the foot of St. Just. He rejoined them on the outskirts of the town.

"Just as well you missed that," he said, wiping the sweat from his brow. "The guard had set up a firing squad and were publicly shooting any known priests or lawyers; I learnt this from the bystanders."

"But how horrible," Magdalena shuddered. "Did no one go to the aid of those unfortunates?"

"That would have been more than their own lives were worth. As far as I could gather orders have been received from Paris for the guards to be more strenuous in their prosecution of the priests and such-like."

"We shall have to be on our mettle to escape their vigilance," Mamselle said in a soft voice.

"I don't think so," Lebrun reassured her. "We look what we are, an itinerant pedlar and his family. The aristos and others who are hunted are those who believe they can affect escape by bribery or fast coaches."

"Let us hope you are correct."

Strangely, with Pierre now of their party, instead of trailing them at a nerve-racking distance, the journey became less arduous. With two men to assist in pulling and pushing the beasts on the road to Grenoble, life was easier for all concerned. Food was still a pressing problem and was more irksome to come by and prepare after the week's respite in the leper-house.

Lebrun suggested, and the others unwillingly agreed, that they should bivouac at night and save themselves running the gauntlet of the villagers or billeted soldiery. After a night or two in the open in some hollow lined with bracken or old leaves, Magdalena came to accept that his advice was sound. The cold surprised her, but when she mentioned this to M. Fourré he told her that each day they climbed a little higher and it was to be accepted that the warmth of the valley would disappear when darkness fell.

The countryside was, indeed, now changing dramatically with hills of considerable size and mountains glimpsed in the far distance. Mamselle seemed to have regained her spirits, and Magdalena forgot the warnings of the kindly nun.

Now and then they encountered other travellers and exchanged greetings, speaking always in country accents and giving no opportunity for anyone to suspect their true identities. When other pedlars or merchants passed them they lingered to barter or buy that ever-essential commodity — food. At farmhouses they sent Pierre to beg for milk and eggs and, on most occasions, he was able to bring a little away with him. At each door he heard the same story of want and shortage, the most pressing problem being the high price of corn.

Fourré considered they were self-assured enough to pass through Grenoble, and they plodded doggedly to Moirans and descended the Isère valley before passing between the magnificent ranges of the Grande Chartreuse and the Bec d'Echaillon, to come across the river and see the forts of the capital of the Dauphiny and the ancient tribe of the Allobroges.

Magdalena was pleased to be in this most beautiful of French cities, for she felt that here, at last, was a tangible link with her past. She knew that it was impossible that Bastien would have remained near his university because Grenoble had been the scene of a revolutionary outbreak as far back as 1788, when a group of citizens had rebelled against Parisian authority and pelted its representative with tiles, thrown from their own roofs.

She was reminded, too, of François, and she began to look forward to the possibility of seeking shelter in his home near Castellane. But was he still alive? Did he still manage to keep his fatherless brood of brothers and sisters in safety? And how were they to find him without drawing suspicion upon themselves?

Grenoble was as lovely as her cousin had told her, nestling as it did in a cup of high snow crowned by mountains, but Fourré had a feeling that it was all too beautiful and calm and, much to Magdalena's annoyance, told his friends that they must push on.

Evening saw them wending their way downhill through forests of chestnuts en route for Gap. On the following morning Mamselle seemed difficult to arouse, but she rallied when Fourré gave her a sip or two of their carefully hoarded cognac. She ate a few mouthfuls of stale bread and allowed Pierre to help her into the saddle. Her face was very pale, and Magdalena was suddenly full of forebodings. The words of the old nun kept ringing in her head ' . . . she'll not last a month if you continue on your way."

For as long as possible they walked beside the river Drac, but as they came to La Mure it was no longer possible to keep by the water, as they were forced to make their way slowly and ever more slowly up the steep gradients of the ancient road. Mamselle was very quiet during this period and often, Magdalena glancing at her, caught her off guard and saw her grimace with pain. She took the opportunity of speaking to Fourré about her concern and he told her grimly that he was as anxious as she was.

"We cannot go back," he said, "so there is nothing for it but to press on and hope."

The next day they covered another twenty or so kilometres, coming half-way to Gap, when Mamselle suddenly fainted and, before anyone could aid her, she slipped to the ground.

Magdalena threw herself from the saddle and gathered the thin form in her arms. "We must stop here! Pierre, see if you can find a ruined barn or shelter where we may stay to rest 'Maman'."

Lebrun climbed the rocky hillside that loomed above the track and came down, amid a shower of pebbles, to say that he could see the roof of some dwelling a short distance further south. Picking Mamselle up as if she were a child, he carried her down the road and waited while Fourré went to the door of the crumbling hovel. When the priest signalled that it was unoccupied he pulled the tired animals to the front of the house, while Magdalena quickly brought bracken and her cloak to make a bed for her governess.

They were, all three, exhausted and hungry, but could not eat. Mamselle did not stir when Fourré lit the lantern. "Sleep if you can," he told Magdalena. "You will be needed to nurse Mamselle when she stirs."

But Mamselle did not move again, and when the first pale light of dawn crept through the unglazed windows of the long-neglected house she quietly slipped away from them into an eternal rest, where she would no longer be forced to sit on the back of an uncompromising donkey, hungry nor pursued by imaginary unnamed faces.

Fourré felt hot tears spring to his eyes as he muttered the last rites over the emaciated woman, and Pierre hastily crossed himself.

"What shall we do?" Fourré asked.

"Bury her before our young mistress wakes," Pierre told him brusquely, and stooped to pick up the body and push his way through the sagging door.

Taking it in turns, he and the priest scooped some sort of shallow grave out of

175

the rocky earth with the spades the groom had insisted they bought in Vienne. It was gruelling and difficult work, for the terrain was hard and the coating of soil slight, while each man laboured with extra determination in an effort to be shot of their grisly task before Magdalena awoke. They decided at last the pit was deep enough, and grunting they covered Mamselle's face with her hood and laid her down in the bare soil which smelt of rotting foliage. They had almost completed their unpleasant task when they heard Magdalena cry out from the hovel.

"I'll go to her while you level the ground and try to make it look as natural as possible," Fourré said, and wiping his brow with the sleeve of his woollen smock went towards the dwelling. He was met at the door by Magdalena, heavy-eyed with sleep and bewildered at finding herself alone.

"Where are you all? Is Mamselle better?"

"You must be brave, my child, but I much regret our dear friend died during the night." As her real father might have done, he put his arm about her shoulder and heard her gasp.

"Oh, *no*! How can I have let her go on when I knew she was so ill? How can I ever forget her kindness and unselfishness? M. Fourré, will I be forgiven?"

"This sadness is not of your causing, Magdalena; your 'mother' would have not had it any other way. She gave her word to those we left behind that she would not abandon her charge."

"I know, I know. That is why it is all so dreadful. If it were not for me, you and she would be living peacefully and quietly at home."

"We cannot be sure of that. You have but to remember the persecution of those of my calling and recall that our dead friend was the daughter of a doctor to realise that when the ignorant masses found their way to our doors we should have been sacrificed with the rest. Until France comes to her senses under the direction of some strong leader the educated are at the mercy of the mob."

Magdalena looked about her. "Where is Pierre?"

"He is putting the finishing touches to the makeshift grave we have dug."

Magdalena's tears began to flow again. "I'll search for a posy of flowers to put on it."

"It would be much better if you did not," Fourré said, full of regret for his young mistress and for himself in the difficult task of bringing her to safety without Mamselle's devotion and common sense. "Anything out of the ordinary might well be investigated by the curious and could lead to all types of questions being asked."

"Then I may, at least, say a prayer over her?"

"Of course."

Pierre was coming towards them, his thin face damp with sweat. "I judge they'll not spot that too easily," he growled.

In fact, so well had he done the job that Magdalena would not have found the site if Fourré had not pointed it out to her. She knelt on the uneven ground, her lips moving in the repetition of the Latin grace and blessing, and allowed Fourré to lead her away to where Pierre was already completing the task of saddling the donkeys and pulling out food from the hamper. "Eat," he commanded in a voice that made Fourré suddenly turn cold. He had never been able to bring himself to trust the fellow implicitly, and he was filled with fear that now Mamselle's restraining influence was gone their uninvited fellow-traveller might take advantage of Magdalena's innocence. Fourré made a mental note never to relax his vigilance. For the first time since they had set out from la Bellefontaine, he was glad that the count had insisted upon him bringing a flint-lock with him. He discovered, in thinking this, he knew no shame as a man of God and hastily fumbled for the rosary he dared not carry, and said several 'Aves' under his breath.

By now the sun was over the mountains to the east and the wood was full of bird-song and the smell of morning freshness. Fourré hustled his companions to finish their bread and cheese and be on their way.

Magdalena was very quiet, unable to think of anything but Mamselle's sacrifice on her behalf. She found herself wondering, not for the first time, who she was that others should give their lives in her service. Looking deeper into the secret reaches of her heart she could see nothing but a vain and selfish girl bent on self-preservation. Yet she was comforted, in some small way, by the fact that she had loved her governess and had tried to make up to her what she had so abundantly given.

During the day they exchanged greetings with their usual quota of northbound voyagers and sold a few lengths of ribbon and a packet or two of pins.

Fourré was now mounted on the other donkey while Pierre walked beside Magdalena. It was he who made the suggestion that they would do well to barter their stock in La Mure for more saleable goods.

"A good idea," Fourré allowed, somewhat grudgingly, "but what?"

"A bale or two of cloth, some sheepskins and stronger shoes: as well as being necessities, the things would be useful to us in an emergency. You can see already that we are going to find

180

very trying conditions ahead of us."

"What do you know of the mountains?" Fourré asked, sharply.

Pierre eyed him for a long moment. "Nothing but what I've gleaned from visiting grooms — those of my lady's cousin and *citoyen* Baron."

There was another pause broken by Magdalena, who turned suddenly to Fourré. "Did you — did you bury 'Maman' just as she was?" These were almost the first words she had uttered since they had left the hovel in the chestnut forest. "I was thinking of how we might buy some more goods, and I remembered."

"Remembered what, my child?" Fourré asked.

"That she always wore a money-belt strapped about her waist." With an effort Magdalena kept her hands from touching her own slender body to ensure that her own corselet was still in place. Having irritated her beyond measure at first, it had now become part of her, and she was used to its reassuring weight. Instinct told her to keep the secret to herself.

"*Mon Dieu!*" Pierre exclaimed. "We cannot leave *that* behind."

"It would be most fitting for me to return and recover it," Fourré said, but his tone implied that he did not relish the descent and the added climb back, neither, in his heart, was he happy at the prospect of leaving his charge with Pierre.

Pierre solved the problem by turning on his heel and calling out that he would rejoin them on the following day. "Don't leave the old road," he shouted, "and then I shall soon overtake you."

The other two watched him until his figure was a blur against the rocky outcrop which overhung the road.

"Well, I hope we shall see him — and the money," Fourré commented drily as he urged his tired mount on the steep upward road.

"Why do you not trust him, *mon père?*"

Fourré shrugged. "I can't tell you: he appears to have our interests entirely at heart, but there is something, *je ne sais quoi*, that causes me disquiet."

Magdalena did not reply. She had

grown up very quickly during the last weeks and she could have told the priest at least one good reason why the groom gave them unstinted service.

They found lodgings for the night in the hamlet of Laffrey: a windswept place with splendid vistas back towards the way they had come, with a distant view of Grenoble, now bathed in the soft light of an early summer sunset.

The inn was primitive, Magdalena's room a shared loft with dirty straw, which she later discovered was well endowed with fleas.

She awoke in the morning tired and longing for the luxury of her marble tub at la Bellefontaine. Sheep's milk and a morsel of unleavened bread did nothing to dispel her disease, and she helped Fourré groom and saddle the donkeys in silence. He, too, was feeling the bite of Mamselle's death and could think of nothing to cheer his companion.

The road onwards did not help, either, for it traversed a bleak upland valley, bordered by lakes but having little other claim to beauty or interest.

"I learnt at the inn that the next place

is a good distance, but that there is an inn of some sort."

"Would it be possible to bathe in one of the lakes?" Magdalena asked. "My clothes are filthy and I itch with flea-bites."

"I'm truly sorry," Fourré muttered, his brow clouded with anxiety, "but there seems nowhere hereabouts to offer privacy."

"Well, let's pray that we find somewhere soon," Magdalena commented, "for if this torment continues I'll be bitten to death before we reach Castellane, let alone Naples."

Fourré laughed, and the sound made them both a little happier.

In the event they did not reach Pierre-Chatel and bivouacked at the southern end of the valley behind a circle of boulders. When they had picked grasses and handfuls of sweet-smelling clover for the donkeys, they ate the last of their cheese and drank from the wine-skins Fourré had replenished at Laffrey. Despite the uncomfortable earth and meagre meal they both fell asleep instantly.

They were awoken at dawn by Pierre, who stumbled into their hiding-place and sank down beside them. Fourré regarded him with badly disguised surprise. Magdalena was strangely relieved for, before he drank or ate, he pulled out his rough shirt and silently handed the money-belt to Magdalena.

"Thank you," she said, quietly, "but *mon père* will take charge of the gold."

"Well enough; it is all there and I left the poor lady to rest at last." He crossed himself involuntarily and drank deep of the wine Fourré proffered.

"You must rest."

"No, if *mon père* will consent to allow me to ride for a time, I shall soon regain my strength."

Magdalena walked beside the priest, and they came, unchallenged, through the hamlet and out onto the road again. They were still on level ground, and their progress was swifter than on any of the days since leaving Grenoble.

They came almost to La Mure as the sun was setting.

"We'd best wait for the morning for the curfew will be enforced by now,"

Fourré commented.

"But I'm so hungry," Magdalena wailed, none of them having eaten since morning.

Pierre looked about him. "There is a flock of sheep yonder and the shepherd is not far off, that is certain. I'll go and seek him out while you find a convenient resting-place."

Above the road a group of pines offered shelter, and after putting the beasts to grass, Fourré and Magdalena wearily pulled themselves up the rocks. To their surprise a waterfall fell in solitary splendour to tumble down towards the road beyond.

Magdalena ran towards the water. "There must be a pool somewhere," she called, and hastily gathering a clean shift and her other crumpled robe she ran off.

Driven by her desire for cleanliness she almost ran up the sheep-track beside the falls and came with delight upon a pool guarded by tumbled boulders of glistening granite.

In minutes she and her soiled garments were in the water, the icy cold a shock after the heat of the day. She could not swim, but she clung to the edge, thrashing her legs about and revelling in the joy of the freedom from clothes and constant travelling. Finding a shallow basin, she stood up and dipped her head under, running her hands through the strands and allowing them to float about her. She forgot everything — the flight, Mamselle's death and the relentless necessity to be constantly on the move — in the sheer delight of the refreshing pool.

Without haste she pulled herself out on to a rock and began to dab herself dry with her clean shift.

A pebble falling into the tranquil inlet made her jump, and she looked up, terrified, to see Pierre regarding her from the opposite side.

His voice calmed her. "Have no fear, Magdalena, I have long thought you the most beautiful woman in France, but I shall not touch you." He turned abruptly and disappeared.

Magdalena hastily put on her clothes and rubbed the ones she had so carelessly thrown upon the waters. How would she be able to face Pierre after this, and what would Fourré say if he knew?

But when she returned to the resting-place, Pierre was cooking pieces of lamb over a fire which Fourré was tending, and the groom paid her no more attention than if it had been an ordinary day.

★ ★ ★

At La Mure they showed their papers, which were stamped after long scrutiny, and made their way down the main street to the square where, after some difficulty, they exchanged all their ribbons and laces for a bolt of kersey and spent one of Mamselle's golden Louis' on a large bundle of fleeces.

One of these Pierre used to cover their worn saddles, and then, having bought wine, cherries and quantities of cheese, they set out for the Col de Bay and the long and dangerous descent to Corps.

Fourré would have lingered at the Roman bridge, and Magdalena would have liked to explore the richly coloured rocks, but Pierre urged them on saying that they had hours of going downhill before they began the tortuous ascent to the Col Bayad and eventually Gap.

"If we ever reach Naples," he said, laconically, "you can indulge your fancies for antiquities and the like in Pompeii and such."

10

IT took them two weeks to pass
through the majesty of the Alps,
with its snow-topped mountains and
flowered-covered valleys. Days of anxiety
as they showed identity papers at
Sisteron, Digne and Barreme. Days
when they suffered hunger, thirst and
sheer exhaustion.

Fourré was no longer stout, and
Magdalena was gaunt, tangle-haired with
her skin tanned with constant exposure
to wind, rainstorms and the omnipresent
sun which daily grew hotter.

Only Pierre seemed unaltered, his thin
face with a little more colour, his stooping
frame hardly changed. Once or twice
Magdalena found him looking at her with
an intensity which made her blush, but
his attitude towards her had not altered
since the incident at the waterfall.

She was to remember the beauty only
long afterwards, when the memory of
clawing her way up almost impossible

heights and the never-ending fight for survival on an empty belly had faded. Several times during the journey Magdalena was to give thanks that Mamselle had died when she did, for she lay, at least, in some kind of peace. If Magdalena found the going almost impossible, it was hard to imagine how the gently reared woman would have faced the task.

One evening in late June the three came down the last tortuous, snake-like mile on the ancient road to Castellane and saw before them the splendid crag crowned by a chapel.

Magdalena sat down on a boulder, holding the bridle of their sole remaining donkey. "I can't believe that we have really come here."

"And now that we have, we are confronted with the problem of finding the estate of M. Baron." Fourré said.

"Well, we won't discover it sitting here," Pierre replied. He helped Magdalena back on to the saddle, and taking the leading rein started off towards the town.

Here the very isolation of the place meant that security was not as strict as in the more northerly towns, and when Fourré told the Republican guard that he and his companions had come from Riez with a bale of sheepskins the man gave a cursory glance at their papers and went back to his hut.

"Quite obvious he can't read," Fourré remarked when they were well out of earshot, "he was holding the papers upside down."

"There can't be anything very suspicious about us by this time," Magdalena said with a sigh.

"That may be," Pierre put in quickly, "but it does not mean that we must relax our guard."

His words were to prove only too prophetic.

★ ★ ★

Fourré considered that Magdalena should spend at least one night in an inn while they found out in which direction lay the estates of François Baron. He saw a suitable establishment in the town square, a small galleried hostelry, outside which several men were sitting drinking; they exchanged surly greetings and went under the arched entrance into the courtyard. Pierre led the donkey to the stables, and Fourré and Magdalena took their bundles and went into the dark interior of the inn.

A thin woman with a pinched expression greeted them and asked their business. Fourré explained that they were pedlars seeking a room. The woman said she could accommodate them in a communal chamber but that food was scarce and she had little to offer but a bowl of soup. Hardly able to conceal her joy at the thought of such a treat, Magdalena asked, "Is there water for washing?"

"There's the pump over by the stable."

Fourré felt a sharp stab of fear as he saw the woman look more closely at the girl, but Magdalena thought no more of it than to thank her and ask when they could eat.

"Help yourself," the woman answered, "the pot is boiling over the fire yonder."

Magdalena stemmed her desire to rush straight to the food and, putting down her bundle on a bench, went to sit outside the inn. Here the evening sun, which had burnt into her skin throughout the day, was sinking. Fourré joined her with three mugs of wine, and when Pierre had finished with the bedding-down of the donkey they relaxed and drank together.

When darkness fell they moved into the common room of the hostelry and took their bowls to fill them with thin gruel. No one made any attempt to engage them in conversation, for these were days of suspicion, and who could tell if innocent-seeming pedlars were not agents of Robespierre's secret police?

Fourré glanced from time to time at the woman who kept the inn and was not completely reassured by what he saw. More than once he opened his mouth to suggest that they finished their meal and went quietly to the stable to take the donkey and vanish into the night. There did not seem much chance of discovering where they would find François Baron's estate from these uncommunicative townsfolk, and it might be easier to make discreet enquiries on the road tomorrow.

The woman disappeared from the long,

low parlour, and her place was taken by a young girl who looked like her daughter. Fourré relaxed and called for another jug of wine.

Magdalena was sleepy and longed to climb the ladder at the end of the room to the bedchambers, but was afraid to go alone. Pierre suddenly leant towards her and Fourré, causing her to be instantly awake. "The man we seek lives a mile to the south of here, in the shade of the rock and by the river."

"How did you discover this?"

"I asked a man who came to the stable while I was unsaddling the beast."

"That was dangerous," Fourré muttered. "How did you know you could trust him?"

"He was leaving the inn and seemed respectable enough, so I felt it was safe enough."

"I hope so."

It was now Pierre's turn to feel apprehensive, and he glanced about him nervously.

"Drink your wine and let's be on our way," Fourré commented.

Magdalena stood up, clutching her

bundle, and moved to the open door as the priest threw some small coins on the table. Pierre pushed past her, and it was he who received the full brunt of the butt of the rifle.

"What the devil!" Fourré exploded, shielding Magdalena and thrusting himself towards Pierre who was staggering, clutching his head.

"Damned aristos! That's what," the innkeeper said, "and I've brought the guard to put you in the lock-up until the morning."

Magdalena, terrified, saw the unkempt soldier who had challenged them earlier and two other men. As she stood behind Fourré she heard Pierre shout out in a voice thickened with pain, "Run for it and leave me to sort out these good-for-nothing rabble."

Fourré hesitated only long enough to see that Pierre was on his feet, and grabbing Magdalena dashed through the circle of Madame and the guards to the safety of the open square.

Her exhaustion now quite forgotten, Magdalena ran after Fourré, hearing footsteps behind her.

"Run as fast as you can and we'll hide in the shadow of the houses beyond."

Dogs were barking and the sound of random musket shot echoed round the empty Place. Magdalena quickened her pace, her chest aching with the difficulty of getting her breath. Quite suddenly Fourré stopped and drew her into an arched doorway. He stooped, picked up a pebble and threw it away from him; a few seconds passed and their pursuer lumbered on past them. As soon as he was gone Fourré glanced up at the heavens, and seeing the outline of the spire-like rock against the brilliance of the star-lit sky, he whispered to Magdalena to move as quietly as possible out of the square and in the direction of the north bank of the river.

In the deserted streets it was easy enough, but once they came close to the Verdon the way became a rutted track which soon began to climb. They moved in silence for a quarter of an hour, and Fourré stopped in the lee of a large boulder. "We are safe for the moment: I imagine they will have expected us to take the bridge."

For a while Magdalena was unable to speak. "What of Pierre?" she asked at last.

"I don't think we need worry about him too much; he will be full of contrition that it may have been he who let slip the information that we were looking for François Baron."

"But that might have been only because we had business with him."

"Yes, of course, I'd not considered that."

Magdalena thought for a moment. "I hope Pierre's remark will not bring harm to François."

"Don't concern yourself about that, because if François is still at his home you can trust that he is accepted by the peasantry. Come, I think I can see lights above us to the left, over there."

Magdalena looked and saw, at some distance, the faint amber glow of lighted windows. She realised with a sinking heart that a wide valley lay between them and what might be their goal.

It took them two laborious hours to descend and climb again until they struck a well-worn, wide path and came to great oaken doors in a high wall.

"Well," Fourré said, "we can but take our chance and, *Mon Dieu*, I pray that we've been guided to the right sanctuary."

While he knocked on the studded panels with his fists Magdalena searched for, and found, the bell-rope which she tugged with the last remnants of her strength. After what seemed a very long time a voice asked who knocked.

"Is this the house of *citoyen* Baron?" Fourré's tone was guarded.

"It is, to his friends."

"Tell him then, that *citoyenne* de la Bellefontaine and her chaplain urgently desire his hospitality."

For the space of minutes nothing happened, and then the two waiting outside heard the drawing of bolts and the turning of keys.

Standing to greet them, with a lantern in his hand, was François. He came quickly to Magdalena, taking her out-stretched fingers in his firm grasp. "Is it really you, *ma belle*? What in the name of God are you doing here? But come in and rest and we can talk later."

"We have another friend still unaccounted for outside," Fourré put in as he heard the bolts being shot once more.

"Then the guard will remain waiting for the rest of the night or until he comes."

The ground beneath Magdalena's feet was uneven and the air redolent of the farmyard. In the light which came from the building in front of her, she could make out a low front door set in a stone wall of great thickness.

François hurried them inside and led Magdalena to an old-fashioned, high-backed chair beside the fire onto which he kicked a huge log.

"Let me look at you," he said to Magdalena as she sank down. "Some wine, Jacques," he called to the man who had been with him at the gate.

"We've been on the run for the last three or four hours," Fourré said.

Remembering that the priest was probably unknown to François, Magdalena introduced him. "We've come a long way together," she went on, "and — "

"You are in great need of an uninterrupted night's sleep. Despite the hordes of my family who still remain beneath the roof of this barn of a place, we have guest-chambers where you can rest. Call Marie," he said to the old man, "she won't mind being awoken to make up beds for such welcome visitors."

"But, are we welcome?" Magdalena asked. "Is it safe for you to harbour fleeing aristos?"

"My position here is as safe as anyone's can be in these troublous times; perhaps you remember my views on equality?" Magdalena nodded, the light from the branched candles making her head swim. "My beliefs have stood me in good stead, and I'm left to farm here much as our family has done for generations. But come, we have days ahead of us in which to talk, I'll show you to your rooms."

Magdalena stood up, swaying, and François, as naturally as if he were her brother, put his arm about her waist and helped her towards the broad staircase and the gallery above.

She was only faintly conscious of a simple, white-walled room and a great bed with a wooden canopy. Without a thought of the modesty Mamselle and Maman had instilled in her, she slipped off her ragged skirt and bodice and climbed between the covers and was instantly asleep.

François rejoined Fourré on the landing. "You are not too tired for a word or two before you retire, Father?"

"Of course not, there is much to discuss."

"Then we'll finish our wine and then you, also, may rest for as long as you wish."

★ ★ ★

Magdalena woke to find sunlight flooding the bed-chamber and to hear the larks trilling not far from the open casement. For a moment or two she could not quite take in the significance of the soft mattress and the touch of the coarse, lavender-scented sheets, and then she remembered the events of the previous evening and was filled with a delicious sense of relief.

Not long afterwards a young girl came in to the room after knocking discreetly on the door. "My brother sent to enquire if you are awake and ready for food."

"How kind of him — I would like to eat, but would be more grateful for some hot water first."

"We have thought of that and have filled in the tub in our room for you." The girl, slim and fair like François, looked curiously at Magdalena. "Is it really true that you have come all the way from the Loire?"

"Quite true," Magdalena grimaced, "and I must look like a gypsy to prove it." She slipped out of bed and followed the girl, who told her that her name was Diane and she was François' third sister.

"You see, there are so many of us that it is quite possible you will have difficulty in remembering who we are!"

"How many of you remain?"

"Half of the girls and the two youngest boys who help François and Jacques in the fields: the others have fled to England and Naples."

"That is my destination; as heiress to my parents they considered it safer for me to flee."

"You must have hated that."

"I did — and do — but when one has been brought up to obedience it is difficult to go against the will of parents, especially when they are kind and good."

They were now in Diane's room, which she obviously shared with a sister. A bath-tub, full of herb-scented warmed water, stood ready.

"Are your mother and father like François?" Diane asked.

"Not quite," Magdalena admitted with an inward chuckle at the thought of her mother's face if she could see the plainness of the Duke's establishment.

"Were they courtiers, then?"

"No, not that, either. My father has liberal ideas, but is a royalist, all the same." She was nonplussed, not knowing if Diane was going out, and longing to sink into the bath. The girl made up her mind for her. "Come on," she said, "the water will be cold, we can talk while you wash." Having a bevy of sisters she was obviously not used to privacy while she bathed.

Never had anything equalled the pleasure

of washing herself from head to toe, and Magdalena dried herself on the bleached bath-sheet, feeling soothed and comforted. Diane gave her creams for her calloused feet and hands and a distillation of flower-oils to rub into her scalp. They had talked all the time Magdalena was bathing and dressing, and Magdalena realised that she had been longing for the talk of women and of her own kind. It was a relief, too, to speak of Mamselle. She poured out the very real guilt and grief she experienced at the loss of her old friend and teacher. "She was so quiet, so good and so self-effacing."

"She never married?"

"Who would have had her? Penniless, not very good looks and a scholar to make matters worse. She should have been a nun and found peace in some abbey."

"Small chance of that nowadays when monks and nuns are guillotined to please the crowds."

"Where will it end?"

"You had better ask François, he knows more of politics than I do. All I'm fit for is making cheese and spinning wool and flax."

But Magdalena was not to see François until the evening, for she later heard that he and one of his brothers had gone into the hills to search for the missing Pierre.

Fourré was full of admiration for the young man. "Not only does he keep this medieval ruin in some form of order but ensures that his siblings are fed and dressed."

Fourré also had bathed, shaved and put on fresh clothing provided by Jacques; he looked ten years younger and already less gaunt. He commented at once on Magdalena's appearance. "Now I shouldn't be ashamed for your mother to see you: it has been a nightmare to watch my gently reared young mistress deteriorate into something little better than a nomad."

Magdalena looked at him quizzically. "But you do not think the experience has been all bad for me, do you?" When Fourré shook his head she went on. "I left la Bellefontaine a self-centred girl with a slight veneer of classical learning to outbalance a prodigious greed for beautiful clothes and jewels. Surely, in my peasant's smock I have come some little way."

"That's certainly true; not only have you travelled hundreds of kilometres of difficult and dangerous country but you have experienced the death of a true friend and managed Pierre's infatuation with masterly skill."

Magdalena rounded on the curé, startled. "How do you know about that?" She had wanted to speak to Diane on the subject but had not known how to do so.

Fourré retorted that it would have been difficult to have missed the looks which Pierre gave Magdalena or misunderstood the willingness with which he undertook any small or distasteful service for her.

"Then you no longer mistrust him?"

"I think not; he had proved himself until last night, and time alone will show if that were a genuine lapse or not."

★ ★ ★

The evening was to see the resolution of any doubts, for François and his brother brought Pierre back from the maquis-covered slopes outside Castellane, where he had lain all night bleeding from a wound in his thigh. Marie was called in from preparing supper to act as nurse, and Pierre was put to bed in a room adjoining that where she and Jacques slept. Before he was given a dose of laudanum Magdalena went with Fourré to visit him. Pierre's long scarred face was ashen and his voice feeble with pain, exposure and loss of blood, but he was able to whisper that he had killed one of the guard and given the other the slip. "Anyway, they have a worn-out donkey for their pains which they'll value more than a scrawny pack of fleeing aristos." Marie led them away.

"He'll do," she said, "but it'll be a couple of weeks before you'll be able to move from here."

Fourré sighed. "I had guessed as much, but it makes me concerned for Mamselle la Bellefontaine."

Marie regarded Magdalena shrewdly. "A bit of a rest won't come amiss, and, *Mon Dieu*, it'll do my poor hard-working young master good to have other company than this crowd of hungry locusts."

* * *

Supper of stewed rabbit, coarse bread and heavy rich red wine was a noisy affair. Each member of the family having something to ask or tell the visitors. Magdalena began to feel quite dazed until she saw François dismiss the brood and heard him ask her to sit with him awhile before retiring.

"Believe it or not I have a room of my own and it waits to welcome you." He led her to a circular chamber which Magdalena guessed was in the tower which stood at one corner of the square, courtyarded house and was both a look-out and a fortress. "What do you think of this hen-run after the elegance of la Bellefontaine?" he asked as he pulled up a leather-backed chair for her to sit on.

"At this moment I think it is paradise."

"You would not hold that opinion if you were here for long or during the winter when winds howl up the valley and wolves come to our very door."

"I don't believe it!"

"You would, if you saw them; but then I hope you never will."

For a minute Magdalena was silent, hurt at his brusque denial of any romantic notions she might have been harbouring. Then, just when she was about to make some caustic comment about real wolves being safer than the men who masqueraded in their clothing as part of the country's present government, he surprised her by bending down and kissing her brow. "God knows, I've been longing to do that ever since that accursed night we first met."

Magdalena felt tears in her eyes, but she blinked them away and began to thank him for taking her and her retinue into his care.

"Did you doubt that I would do anything else? I would go to the guillotine for you."

"But you do not love me?" The question was wrung out of her, almost mechanically.

"I did not say that, but there never has been and never can be any future life for you and me." He knelt at her side, and taking her hand cradled it against his cheek. "If this is love, I *do* love you; I've never felt it for any other woman and never shall, but my first devotion — and my sacred duty — is to the well-being of this estate and those who depend upon me. There is no room for the overwhelming passion which would develop and devour me if you were to become my wife. Anyway, how could a gentlewoman like you take to the harsh realities of existence in this mountain wilderness?"

"I seemed to have weathered a considerable journey during the past weeks," Magdalena murmured.

"And I'm full of admiration for that feat, but you were driven on by self-preservation. Here it would be a constant fight against poverty with each boring day convincing you that you had been a fool to throw away the chance of the life you deserve as the wife of a rich nobleman."

"How can you be sure of that?"

He turned to look at her, staring for a long time into her eyes. "Because I know human nature and realise that your parents have other plans for their heiress than to marry a penniless duke who lives in squalor."

"But the house is beautiful," Magdalena protested. "I've walked about it this afternoon and see that it has a grandeur all its own; there is something of the past, some air of the reality of life through the ages that is missing at la Bellefontaine."

"That's as maybe, for your home is new by these standards, but think of the luxury you enjoy."

"*Enjoyed*. Yes, I think of that often and wonder how *ma mère* and *mon père* are faring."

"I'll send Jacques to find out."

"Oh, no, that's most kind of you, but I couldn't bear to think of him travelling alone all that way. When I arrive in Naples, if I ever do, perhaps word will have come by sea. If not, I'll send Pierre by ship to Bordeaux and hope he reaches the Loire in safety."

"Have you news of Bastien?"

"None, have you?"

"No, so we shall have to hope he is safe somewhere."

"Where are your brothers?"

"They have also gone to the court of the Two Sicilies at Naples."

"Then perhaps I shall meet them. What are their names?"

"Matheus and Jean-Claud, and if you do I shall think they are the luckiest fellows in the world." He stooped and kissed her again, very tenderly, on the cheek. "Now you must go to bed and rest for you still have a long way to travel."

Magdalena bit back the retort that if she stayed at his château she need never venture on the road again because she realised that François loved her but not in the way she had hoped and perhaps, who knew, she did not really understand what love was herself.

11

THEY stayed at François' home for two weeks; during which time their host was unfailingly helpful, and they all recovered their health and strength.

Magdalena and François became good friends, managing to find time each evening when the others were about their own affairs to sit together and talk of everything and anything which came into their minds. The book-lined walls of the turret retreat heard discussions differing from arguments about life after death to the absurdities of some of the customs of the old court which had led to the downfall of the King.

"I heard that one of the ladies had her hair dressed with her own chemise and went into a ball without realising what a dreadful sight she was!"

"And did you hear of that charlatan Dr. Mesmer? He had a consulting-room in the Place Vendôme where he placed a bucket filled with glass and water from which long tubes of metal protruded — it looked something like a spider. Those afflicted with pains in the stomach, eyes, ears or chest were instructed to clutch a rod and place their other hand on the site of their troubles while gazing at the water."

"Did it cure anyone?" Magdalena asked.

"Apparently, but it is quite possible they would have recovered anyway."

It was not only from François that Magdalena gleaned knowledge. Diane and the other girls gave her her first lessons in housewifery. She who had never held a needle in her hand other than for embroidery was taught the rudiments of darning, patching and spinning. Magdalena found the last the most soothing and interesting of her new skills and was further instructed in the art of knitting. "We don't want to make a *tricoteuse* of you, but you never know when any small accomplishment will be of use."

"If I succeed in delivering my letter of introduction to Queen Marie Carolina I imagine all I've learnt will be needed, for her family is larger than your own, isn't it?" Magdalena answered with a smile.

Marie was also glad of an extra pair of willing hands in her vast and airy kitchen close to the gatehouse.

"Those young madames of mine will be only too glad to slink off to the cherry orchard and idle their time while you do their jobs, but you are supposed to be resting."

"Oh, I'm quite recovered now, a week in the care of this family has ensured that! I wish I could stay for ever."

"Humph," Marie grunted, "you've not had long enough to know what you're saying."

★ ★ ★

When it became apparent that Pierre's leg was sufficiently healed to allow them to leave the château and begin the final part of the journey through the Alpes Maritimes to the sea, François told Fourré and Magdalena that he was sending one of his shepherds with them as far as Grasse. "His family have served mine for generations and he is to be trusted completely: his knowledge of the mountains is without equal and he will take you by the easiest route."

"There are still many kilometres to cover," Fourré remarked, "do you think *ma petite maîtresse* will be able to walk them?"

"I don't intend that she should try: neither can Pierre be expected to travel far on his wounded leg. We've plenty of donkeys, and three won't be missed."

"But we could not possibly take them from you! Would you allow us to pay for them and for our keep while we have been your guests?"

"You mean you have gold with you?" François' voice was incredulous. "How in the name of God have you been able to keep that a secret all this time? Any passing traveller with an inkling of booty would have murdered you in broad daylight for a single louis."

"We were extremely careful to pay only with small *monnaie* which we received in exchange for the goods we pedalled. Bribery was often in my mind, but I always rejected the idea as being the last resort of a coward," Fourré replied.

"If it is not impertinent, may I ask how you accomplished this ideal?"

Magdalena blushed. "Mamselle and I wore kidskin money-belts about our waists, and when my chaperone died my adopted father took over her responsibility."

François laughed. "Mamselle was not large if I remember; it must have been a tight squeeze to put that girdle round your sturdy figure, Fourré!"

"My figure was not so sturdy then, Monsieur, and a little stretching here and there sufficed. But, come, we refuse to take the donkeys without paying for them."

"Well," François was obviously torn. "I would give you anything, but something towards Diane's dowry would certainly not go amiss."

Magdalena looked at him and, taking courage, asked the question which had been in her mind for some time. "Would Diane like to go with us?"

"Diane must answer that question herself," François replied.

But when Diane was confronted with the question she told her new friend quietly that she had promised her dead mother that she would remain at the château while she was needed and until her next sister was old enough to take her place. "You see, there is also someone I hope to marry who lives not far from here at the other end of the Verdon gorge, and, one day, when the Terror has died down, we may be able to marry."

"I'm sorry for myself," Magdalena confessed, "but hope with all my heart that the day is not far distant when you may do as you wish."

★ ★ ★

Magdalena and François spent their last evening together walking on the battlements in the stillness of the warm summer evening. "How can I ever thank you?" she enquired.

"I need no thanks; these weeks have been the happiest of my life and the memory of them will stay with me for ever."

Magdalena turned to face him and, putting her arms about his shoulders, kissed his mouth. For a long moment he did nothing but savour the sweetness of her embrace, and then with a groan he grasped her tightly and covered her face and neck with kisses. Then suddenly he pushed her away from him. "Don't," he pleaded, "my life is almost intolerable at this moment and another minute of this madness will ruin both of us. Go to bed while I've still the willpower to resist you."

Magdalena, more pragmatic than when she had come under François' roof, murmured a quick goodnight and slipped away to her bedroom. Here she slept, soundly enjoying what she knew would be the last trouble-free night she would experience until she might come to Naples.

★ ★ ★

Soon after dawn in the cold, musty chapel of the château, Fourré celebrated mass using bread and wine from the kitchen and cellar. It was a sober gathering which partook of the sacrament, and later when breakfast was finished the household made their farewells.

Diane was in tears, the other girls sniffed, and François said little or nothing. Marie, the most practical of them all, handed Pierre a small rush basket of food. "This'll keep you going for a day or two."

Only François came to the gate, and he did not linger for fear that any observer might make overmuch of a shepherd and his family setting out for new pastures. But he stayed in the window of his turret-room until he could no longer distinguish the slow-moving party, then he leant against the old glass and wept.

* * *

At about the same time as Magdalena was leaving Castellane, six ships from Lord Hood's Mediterranean Fleet were watering at Cadiz, that white-walled Moorish town, west of Gibraltar. Here the Spaniards, who regarded the events in France with horror, set themselves out to entertain the officers and men from the trim British ships with lavish courtesy.

The Captain of the *Agamemnon*, a certain Horatio Nelson, went aboard the

Spanish Admiral's *Concepcion* and was royally entertained to a long and exotic feast. When this was over he was driven through the quiet, sunset-flushed streets to a rocky island where he was joined by his first Lieutenant and other junior officers.

Here in an amphitheatre which held 16,000 noisy men and women, the English were expected to enjoy the spectacle of a first-rate bull-fight. In vain it was explained to the frail-looking Captain that no one in Spain would miss such an opportunity, for he felt sick and was certain his fellow officers were also suffering. It was true that the picadors, matadors and toreadors, in their brilliant clothes and scarlet cloaks, were picturesque and, to judge by the rapturous applause, very highly esteemed; their shapely calves and strutting stances would have graced any London stage, but the goading of the helpless bull into bellowing misery, the goring of the horses and their subsequent slaughter was sufficient to turn the stomachs of men who were prepared to grapple and board an enemy vehicle. They were more than delighted when, after what seemed an eternity, the fight was over and they could return to their ship.

Captain Nelson's ship was slightly different from those of his fellow Captains, for, though he had been only recently recalled to service after five years at home in Norfolk, he had forgotten nothing of the twenty years he had served in the Navy. All his men were in dress of a similar type; blue jackets, bell trousers, a handkerchief at the neck and a black-painted straw hat. Captain Nelson believed that discipline meant happiness, and his ship had been besieged with old-timers when commissioning.

The weather at the outset from the Nore had been foul, with gales and high seas. Now as they provisioned and took on wine at Gibraltar, the sun shone endlessly and the company settled down to run for the waters outside Toulon where they had heard thirty French warships were preparing to put to sea.

According to Nelson the battleships were enormous, with double the number of his guns, but, despite this, Lord Hood sent in a flag of truce for the exchange of prisoners. When nothing came of this move and the French showed no sign of leaving port to challenge the much smaller English fleet, the Commander-in-Chief sailed along the coast keeping a watchful eye for a stray merchantman of the enemy or a frigate on patrol, but they saw nothing.

In view of this, *Agamemnon* was allowed to come close inshore and the English had their first sight of French territory. It seemed deserted, no traffic on the dusty roads and endless miles of pines and olive-groves. An occasional glimpse of a sandy beach made several of the ship's company long to stand on solid land, but the rumour in Spain had been of a guillotine set up in nearby Marseilles and the inhabitants of Provence drunk with blood-madness and starved of food. The risk of putting out a jolly-boat was too great.

In the light of this knowledge, it came as something of a shock when Lord Hood was approached by the Commissioners of Marseilles, who begged for a truce. The representatives from the town passed on the unbelievable news that the French fleet would remain at Toulon; their Commanders preferred the mercy of the English to the rapacious demands on life and property by the Republicans.

Just as Nelson and his officers were preparing to go about and enter Toulon, he received orders from Lord Hood that *Agamemnon*, being a fast sailer, was to carry despatches to Italy and letters for the hands of the British envoy to the court of the Two Sicilies at Naples.

If most of the ship's company were disappointed, two, at least, were fuming at their ill-luck: Josiah Nisbet, Captain Nelson's stepson who, at thirteen, suffered from overpowering sea-sickness, and George Gates, the most junior watch-keeping officer on board, who, despite his years at sea, had never before been in the Mediterranean and was now snatched from realising a life-long ambition.

* * *

François' shepherd led Magdalena and her companions over sheep-tracks to the Col de Luens and brought them by easy stages through La Foux to Malamaire, Andon, Pont de Loup and finally after yet another tedious climb through the Cal de la Sine to Grasse.

Here, where since the time of Catherine de Medici, scent had been made from wild mimosa, carnations, roses and jasmine, the shepherd left them. By this time they had all seen enough to realise that the situation of the inhabitants of Southern France was as bad, if not worse, than anywhere else in the country. Fourré had even heard whispers of counter-revolution which were louder than any he had encountered before. If Civil War broke out the danger to his young charge would be greater than ever.

It was at Grasse, also, that Magdalena had her first glimpse of the sea. From a thousand feet up she could see a wide expanse of pale turquoise water that gave her a thrill of pleasure. She was not sorry then when Fourré gave his opinion that they should make all haste for the little fishing-port of Nice. Pierre, who was subdued since his wounding, agreed with this advice and said that he would make it his business to arrange passage for Naples.

"If you will entrust me with some of the gold I'll be less suspect than either M. Fourré on his own or all three of us together."

They agreed that this was a good plan, neither Fourré nor Magdalena doubting that the money would be perfectly safe with the groom; he had, after all, had hundreds of opportunities of taking their hidden wealth ever since he had undertaken to return and retrieve Mamselle's share.

It was Magdalena who caused them to pull up abruptly a few moments after they had taken the road for the port. "I remember now! François told me to think twice before choosing Nice for our departure because the Republicans will almost certainly have destroyed the bridge over the Var: he told me it had been blown up three times in his lifetime."

"Where did he suggest we sailed from?" Fourré asked.

"I think he said Antibes."

"But when he and I discussed the

matter he assured me that Nice was a larger port and we should have more choice of vessels."

"Well, that settles it," Magdalena said, "only for the love of Our Lady let us be on our way."

They spent the night, huddled in their sheepskins, in an ancient round stone house used for centuries by itinerant goat herds and probably once the house of pre-Christian inhabitants of La Colle Loubière.

Magdalena was restless, sleeping fitfully, and she knew that Pierre was suffering with his leg. Only the old priest slept soundly; soon after dawn Magdalena woke him saying that her cramped limbs could no longer endure the hardness of the packed-earth floor.

By the time they approached Caques, passing beneath the walls of several villages perched precariously on the hills above them, it was already uncomfortably hot.

"Before we come to the bridge — if it still stands — it would be as well to be rid of the donkeys," Fourré suggested. "Even if we can't sell them, at least we can make out they were the source of the money we shall offer to the ship's master."

Between Haut-de-Caques and the main village they passed a low farmhouse building where a wizened old man was leading two thin cows out to a rocky pasture. He regarded the trio with fear until they asked him if he had cheese or an egg or two.

"What'll you pay for it, if I have?"

"One of the donkeys," Fourré replied, looking steadily at the Provencian.

"One of the donkeys?" he echoed, incredulous.

"You can have them all if you've some cooked meat and some figs or peaches."

The old man stared, hit the cows with the switch he carried to ease his amazement and shouted to an equally shrivelled old woman, who stood watching half-in, half-out of the farmhouse door. She beckoned her man, and after a minute's consultation Magdalena and the others were called inside.

Flustered, the old crone motioned to a bench in the cool kitchen and set before them wooden platters and pottery mugs. With quick, bird-like movements which belied her age, she produced a coarse pâté, bread and a passable home-made wine.

Although their patois was almost unintelligible it transpired that they and their forebears had farmed the place for generations. The land was owned by a marquis who had long since fled and they paid no rent to anyone.

"Are you not afraid of the Republicans?"

Madame's face was a study of canny common sense. "We side with no one and can usually find a bite for Girondists and rebels alike: curse them all, we say, and let us live out the rest of our lives in peace."

"We've heard nothing but stories of starvation," Pierre remarked.

"Mostly from good-for-nothing idlers, I'll be bound."

"Not always," Fourré murmured. "Is the bridge repaired?"

"No, if you want to cross over you'll have to be carried."

When they left, carrying only their

bundles, they had refilled the basket Marie had given them, and they left two gaping peasants staring after them like unbelievers on a medieval frieze.

When Magdalena saw the river she wished they had gone to Antibes for, though not wide, it was running very fast. However, she could do nothing but accept the offer of being carried across on the shoulders of the stalwart villagers who, obviously enjoying their task, told her to close her eyes in case she became giddy and fell into the water.

Once over she laughed in sheer relief as her two friends were brought to her side. "My mother would die of horror," she said, and immediately fell silent, remembering that she had almost forgotten the patrician features of Maman and the benevolent face of her father.

★ ★ ★

They came to the old city which had its origins in the mists of a Greek occupation two thousand years before and came to the new harbour of Lympia lying in the shadow of the castle.

"I wish to God this place still belonged to the kingdoms of Sardinia," Fourré said, and led them to a waterfront inn. "Drink up, Pierre, and set about finding a ship as soon as you're able."

"You are nervous?" Magdalena asked as Pierre disappeared.

"Yes, but that is inevitable when a goal is almost reached; our safety is more in danger at this moment than at any other time."

But Magdalena refused to echo his sombre reflections because she could not believe that the good God who had brought them so far and through so many trials would desert them at the eleventh hour.

She was proved right, for after an hour's absence Pierre returned to say that he had found a captain willing to take passengers with his cargo of scents and ceramics to Naples.

"I think he guessed the reason for the voyage, but the sight of the gold coins dispelled any doubts on where his sympathies lay. He grumbled at the chaotic state of Nice but did allow that it was an ill wind which blows no good, for Grasse scent-makers usually use Marseilles to ship their wares abroad but are afraid to go there at the moment."

The three walked round to the other side of the harbour and walked a narrow gangplank to a two-masted ship lying tied to the wharf: she seemed very small to Magdalena.

The master, a short dark man with the build of an ox, greeted them and hurriedly showed them below. "The accommodation is rough," he told them, "but I sail with tomorrow's dawn and you'll not do better than that."

"But there are only two bunks!" Magdalena cried as the master disappeared up the companion-way to the deck.

"Yes, milady," Pierre said, quietly, "this is the end of my journey."

"You can't leave us now!"

"I've accomplished what I set out to do, which was to bring you safely to the coast and with that accomplished I'll return to la Bellefontaine with the good news."

Fourré regarded him. "You won't try to retrace our route here?"

"No, I'll find a ship — if there are any available to Bordeaux."

"I can't believe it," Magdalena cried. "You've become part of the 'family'."

"That is just the problem, milady. While we were travelling we were as one, but when, once you reach the Court of Naples, you will be again a great lady and I but a humble groom: for M. Fourré it is different. This is the better way, believe me, I've given it much thought."

Magdalena was stunned, but when she realised Pierre was in earnest she said that he must have money. "And what of letters for my parents?"

"I would rather carry messages than take the written word, milady: if I'm searched they'll find only the gold and they'll believe me if I tell them I stole it from an aristo."

Once he had broken the news he begged to be excused and said that he would put up at the inn opposite for the night and would not depart until he had seen them, sails hoisted, and safely on their way.

After he had gone Magdalena slumped

down on to the narrow berth and stared blankly at Fourré. "Will there ever come a day when there'll be no more partings?" she asked at last.

"I pray so," the priest sighed.

12

THE weather held fair and the water, which could be whipped into sudden furies by a shift in the wind, stayed a placid calm as they left France behind them and stood out to hug the coast of Italy through the Ligurian sea. Two days out, passing between the northern finger of Corsica and the island of Elba, Magdalena and Fourré were sitting opposite each other propped up against the cabin top and the rails. A good breeze filled the sails and the vessel cut through the wavelets at a good pace.

Magdalena sat with her head back and her eyes closed: Fourré looked at her, considering the change which had taken place since they had fled from la Bellefontaine and liking what he saw. The girl's dark hair had bronze lights from constant exposure to the sun, and her complexion, which had been on the pale side, was glowing with golden colour. It was true that she was thinner, but in some strange way this added, rather than detracted, from her pervasive beauty. The long, tapering fingers were engrained with dirt and her feet, bare on the warm deck, were calloused and unkempt, but still graceful.

Yet, although he approved of this shift in Magdalena's attraction, the old priest knew that the alteration was more than skin deep.

Fourré found himself wondering how she would adapt to court life: although her mother had enjoyed it, the count was never happy in the confining atmosphere of protocol.

It was, perhaps, fortuitous that the rumours coming out of the Palaces of Naples spoke of a very different mode of life from that which had provoked the rebellion in Paris against the Queen's sister.

Ferdinand, now forty-two, was the third son of Charles III of Spain and had been King of Naples and Sicily since he was eight. His elder brothers had both inherited the family insanity, and to guard Ferdinand from this omnipresent threat his mentors had been told to keep him from study and allow him to hunt and enjoy himself.

Ferdinand, like any boy before or since, revelled in this leniency and now hunted and shot any living creature on the slightest excuse and mixed with his Neapolitan subjects as if he were their blood-brother: Fourré had heard that he was very popular and even sold fish on the quay-side.

It followed that someone had to govern the country, and this task fell to Maria Carolina who was not the daughter of the late Empress Marie Theresa for nothing. Early in her marriage she had borne a son and immediately claimed her right to participate in the Councils of State. Ferdinand was only too delighted to leave it to her and almost always followed her advice. Fourré had also been informed by the count that the Queen had a most capable minister in one John Acton, an Englishman, who had made his home in Naples. "Some say," the count had told Fourré, "he is her lover. There may be truth in it for she has at least fourteen children, but gossip will always improve upon truth and I doubt that the King, if he had his own dalliances, would permit the Queen the same licence."

The skipper of the small ship and his two hands were from Monaco, the small princedom east of Nice, a fact which Fourré and Magdalena found comforting although not completely allaying their fears that they might well be murdered for the contents of their bundles: corsairs were all too well known on the uninhabited coasts through which they were passing.

Food, though badly cooked, was plentiful, and when Magdalena offered to help in the galley the gesture, temporarily overshadowed at least her obvious physical allure. Coping with a small charcoal burner set in an iron frame was no easy task, but the broiled fish was tasty, and a less restrained atmosphere prevailed among the ship's company after they had all eaten her first meal.

Fourré and Magdalena slept in a tiny cabin in the fo'c'sle, and the priest, with her permission, took the precaution of locking the rickety door each night and placing the small firearm, primed, near at hand.

In the event the crew proved to be more interested in landing their cargo safely than in rape and murder, and they came into the Bay of Naples at dusk with the westering sun glittering on the windows of the mounting terraces of the city and casting a rosy glow on the towering peak of Vesuvius.

While the master and his men made preparation to furl the sails and come alongside the harbour walls, Fourré and Magdalena made themselves as presentable as possible. When they were safely moored Fourré paid over the last of the promised money and, making their farewells, followed Magdalena up a flight of stone steps to the quay. Here all was pandemonium with men, women and children milling about talking, shouting, cursing and pushing one against another. Fourré was mobbed, and a crowd of *ragazzi* clustered round Magdalena begging for a coin; she fumbled in the drawstring purse at her waist and, throwing a few sous, escaped to Fourré's side. With some difficulty the priest made it understood that they required a conveyance. At once everyone's brother had just the right cart or wagon, but after considerable delay Fourré succeeded in forcing his way up from the harbour to the Via Caracciola where under a street lamp he spotted a priest in a dusty soutane. This worthy was able to impart the knowledge that the King might be at the Palazzo Reale, but the Queen was at Portici. Hackney carriages, he said, could be hired outside the Teatro S. Carlo which was close by the royal house: he vaguely indicated a direction and shuffled off to be instantly surrounded by beggars and a horde of small children.

Fourré took Magdalena's hand, and together they walked the crowded pavements and came up the slope to the Opera House. A row of broken-down carriages stood waiting, Fourré approached the first. "It's not very clean," he said.

"That won't worry me," Magdalena shrugged. "I'm not very clean either and I'm worried that the Queen will not recognise me as being the daughter of her sister's courtier."

"I don't think that should worry you — besides, you have your mother's letter."

"If it has not disintegrated during the journey!"

Fourré told the driver, who regarded them with open curiosity, that they wanted to go to Portici.

"But that's five miles from here."

"Well, you'll take us all the same," Fourré said testily.

"I'll want to see your money first."

"You'll see that the moment you put us down at the entrance," Fourré's face was darkening.

"*Per favore*," Magdalena pleaded, and was rewarded with a smile and flick of the whip to the two, thin-shanked horses.

For most of the way the hackney was besieged by beggars, and at one congested street corner two ragged boys succeeded in clambering over the back. Now, somewhat surprisingly, the driver took pity on his ill-dressed passengers and turned to threaten the children. Calling out a string of expletives the urchins tumbled into the filthy roadway, and they continued on their lumbering way.

Afterwards, Magdalena was to admit

that the hour and a half's ride to the Queen's residence was the most anxious time of her flight; what awaited them at the end?

It was quite dark when at last the driver reined in under the shadow of a huge building which straddled the highway. "Here you are then and I hope you're in luck."

Fourré, aching in every limb, paid what seemed an exorbitant sum and led Magdalena to the main entrance where flambeaux lit the warm night.

Two sentries stood on guard, and at Fourré's request one went into the hall and summoned a footman. This well-dressed individual took one look at them and told the sentry that beggars were not allowed within the Palace.

"But we are not beggars," Magdalena said, "I have letters for her Majesty from my mother, la comtesse de la Bellefontaine."

The footman looked more closely at the girl, and then, grudgingly, bade them be seated and took Magdalena's note, which she had kept to that day around her waist in the money-belt, and placed it on a silver salver.

He was gone for half an hour or more and Magdalena was sure they had been forgotten, but he reappeared down a magnificent carved marble staircase and asked them to follow him. As they did so Magdalena saw a beautiful woman in a dress of gauzy-silk spangled with stars come out of a door hidden in some panelling, cross the hall and go out to a waiting carriage. Magdalena was suddenly aware that she was totally out of place in such company and amid such elegance, and with her foot on the first stair turned to run out of the building.

"*Mon Dieu!*" Fourré exclaimed. "What's this?"

"I can't go in — they'll laugh at me."

"Oh no, they'll not do that. Put your trust in God and all will turn out well. We've not come all this way to have you shying at the last fence."

Reluctantly Magdalena came back to the foot of the stair and slowly began to climb.

★ ★ ★

In a small anteroom they were met by a woman of about thirty, dressed simply but fashionably, and by a man who introduced himself as the Queen's major domo. "Her Majesty presents her compliments and has read the letter penned by Madame la comtesse de la Bellefontaine and, although she has been plagued by a stream of refugees seeking her charity, she is prepared for her unfortunate sister's sake (May God comfort her in her distress) to make an exception in Mamselle's case — "

"Her Majesty is also led to believe," the woman interrupted, "that you have brought funds with you which will make you independent." Her look denied that she agreed with this possibility.

Fourré, bowing first to Magdalena, agreed that that was indeed the case and neither he nor milady would be a drain on the purse of the household.

The woman brightened. "Then you are most welcome. The Queen, who is expecting her sixteenth child quite shortly, begs me to ask you to excuse her from an audience this evening. She will, however, be delighted to receive you at noon tomorrow."

"That would be an honour," Magdalena murmured, "but I regret that unless you have a sempstress who can fashion a gown overnight I shall have to postpone paying my respects."

The woman looked Magdalena up and down. "Yes, I can understand your reluctance and doubtless after a long journey you will find your clothes somewhat creased."

Magdalena laughed. "Madame, what you see now is the sum total of our wardrobe."

"Indeed? I can well understand that fleeing from these wretched Jacobins — who have tried to establish themselves here, I might tell you — it was necessary to wear a disguise, but there must have been room in your conveyance — "

Fourré stopped her. "La comtesse and I have come by donkey and foot, madame, from the upper reaches of the Loire and we carried as little as possible."

"But that is incredible! Forgive me, I had not understood." She turned to Magdalena. "If you will follow me I'll see that you have a pleasant room and an opportunity to rest."

The major domo took Fourré with him, and Magdalena, reluctant to be parted from the priest, went with the waiting woman through a pair of magnificent doors to a long gallery which ended with a smaller door. "We're now in the Queen's private apartments — I hope you are fond of children for they're everywhere, I'm afraid."

"Children will be a pleasure after the company in which I've mixed of late."

The woman showed her into a square room with a marble floor and a bed hung with curtains of fine net. "I expect you would like to wash so I'll see that water is brought, and as for clothes, it should be simple enough to find something of the Queen's; she is so often pregnant that her wardrobe is full of unworn dresses."

"That would be most kind," Magdalena said, putting her grimy bundle down on a brocade-covered chair.

"Would you like a personal maid?"

"That would be very nice; I've almost forgotten what it is to be waited on."

"There are plenty of young girls only too anxious for employment; Naples has a teeming population of idle creatures and the Palace never seems to be short of willing help. You can pay her?"

"Yes, of course, but the amount M. Fourré (who was our curé) and I've managed to bring is not vast."

"It'll probably be enough by our standards, and this terrible régime in France surely cannot last for ever."

"That is our prayer," Magdalena agreed, and then asked if it were possible to find out if any letters had arrived for her from her parents.

"I know nothing of any correspondence, but it is possible that the Queen's secretary might have something for you."

"Oh, that would be wonderful. It is over three months since we left my house and I long for news."

The woman turned to leave her. "I'll have some supper sent up for you."

"Thank you, it will be a pleasure to eat in a civilised manner." She hesitated. "Madame, may I ask, is the court very formal? I saw a most beautiful girl dressed with such elegance that I'm almost afraid to appear."

"Who was that I wonder? Oh, but of course, that would be Emma Hamilton, the wife of Sir William Hamilton, the British Ambassador. You've no need to worry, she's a great friend of the Queen's and likes dressing up above all else; the rest of us tend to be less fashionable."

"That comes as something of a relief."

A little later five or six dark-eyed girls carried in a wooden tub which they filled with warm water from large stone jars. They regarded Magdalena with curiosity, but did not forget to pay her the courtesies of a station which they had had explained to them but which they could hardly believe.

They did not speak French, but the similarities of the two languages enabled them to understand one another well enough.

A small, fragile girl with dark eyes and olive complexion brought a morning-robe of thin muslin, a pile of delicate underwear and a more formal gown of rose-coloured silk. Magdalena gathered that she was offering her services and accepted them gladly, happy to have female companionship once again.

★ ★ ★

Despite the luxury of the bath and excellence of supper Magdalena could not sleep in the curtained comfort of the bed. Her mind was on fire with the events which had finally culminated in her safe arrival at Maria Carolina's court. Pathetic pictures of Mamselle jostled the bitter-sweet memories of her stay at François' house. Had she perhaps been foolish to have left his château? Would it not have been a possibility that after more time in her company his reserve would have broken? Yet, some instinct told her that she did not really love the strange, idealistic young man, and once having made the conquest she might have lived to rue the day.

She thought of her mother and father and of Pierre making the wearisome return journey and prayed he would find a ship. She thought, most of all, about M. Fourré and wondered where he was in this cavernous palace. She fell asleep just before dawn, hoping it would not be too long before she was reunited with her old friend and confessor.

She slept until noon and woke to find the little maid patiently sitting, sewing, by the shuttered window. The girl was on her feet the instant Magdalena stirred.

"What time is it?"

"*E suonata mezzogiorna, signorina.*"

"Midday! But that is terrible."

"You were very tired, *signorina*. Would you like some hot chocolate?"

"Yes please, what is your name?"

"Bianca, *signorina*."

When Bianca went away, Magdalena dressed quickly, enjoying the delight of slipping on a fine cambric shift and the delicate morning-dress. It was a relief to be without the money-belt which she had carefully hidden in one of the tall vases that flanked the fire-place.

After she had had her breakfast the lady-in-waiting knocked and said she had come to enquire if Magdalena had all she needed. "Her Majesty will receive you before dinner which will be at six o'clock."

"Thank you," Magdalena said, "I shall be ready." She hesitated. "M. Fourré, would it be possible to see him soon?"

"M. Fourré? Ah, your priestly friend; yes, I'm sure that can be arranged. There is a small salon immediately outside the door of the Queen's apartments; I'll arrange for him to be there in just over an hour."

★ ★ ★

Fourré was almost unrecognisable in clean clothes and his hair and beard washed and trimmed. "You look better already," he said, beaming.

Magdalena sighed. "Yet I could not sleep."

"Neither could I, but that will pass. You have not yet seen the Queen?"

Magdalena shook her head.

"No, nor I the King: he is selling fish at the quayside and buying new hunters and is not expected back until tonight. I hear from some of the Queen's gentlemen that his Majesty would spend all day, every day, in the delights of the chase or with his people at the harbour, but the Queen insists he spends some time on affairs of state. Apparently Maria

Carolina is terrified that the populace will rise against the royal household."

"That's understandable with her sister in prison and her brother-in-law beheaded, yet there didn't seem to be much of the Jacobin element in the crowd we saw yesterday."

"No, certainly not, and Ferdinand is highly thought of for his lowly habits; all the same she has sent to the English Navy for protection and promised she will provide troops in exchange."

"But is the English fleet here? They are a long way from home."

"They are at war with France, Magdalena, and France stretches from the Channel south to the Mediterranean."

"Then perhaps we have fled from one terror only to succumb to another."

"I don't think so." They talked for an hour or so and made arrangements to meet every day at the same time.

Magdalena was disappointed to discover that Fourré had been unable to trace any letters from la Bellefontaine, neither was Bastien known at court although someone thought he had heard of François Baron's two younger brothers.

She was not sure what she expected of Maria Carolina, but when she was presented at the appointed time she found the forty-one-year-old Queen a regal enough figure. Stout with much childbearing, her Hapsburg nose gave her a somewhat daunting appearance, but when Magdalena made her curtsy she acknowledged the salute and beckoned her to come nearer.

Magdalena was aware of many children, a man of striking good looks standing at the Queen's side and the same woman she had glimpsed in the hall on the previous evening sitting near by. "So you are come from my poor bereaved sister's country." Tears filled the small eyes. "I've heard many stories, all of them fearful, but am anxious to have your latest news. Come and sit with me and tell me if you have any hopes for the future."

Magdalena told her as best she could of the past months with its privations and experiences. The Queen listened attentively, turning more than once to the handsome man beside her. When Magdalena had finished she said, "So, *mon enfant,* you have lived to reach our court in safety for which *le Bon Dieu* be thanked." She spoke to the good-looking man who had been listening attentively. "And I think we are right, Sir John, to ask for the protection of the English men-of-war and prepare our mercenaries for action." The Queen held out her hand to Magdalena. "You must be exhausted with your travels, so we shall not expect you to attend upon us for a week."

"That is most kind," Magdalena murmured. "May I thank you for your courtesy in receiving me."

Maria Carolina waved expressive hands. "You are most welcome, and when you are rested you'll have enough to do, I promise. Before you go may I take this opportunity of presenting you to my two good friends, English both. Sir John Acton, my chief adviser, and Lady Hamilton, the wife of the English Envoy — she is my *confidante* and brought me my last letter from my poor threatened sister."

Magdalena curtsied to the elegant, cool man and the lovely young woman who responded to her salute with a warm smile and an open expression of admiration for her good looks. Magdalena blushed, but the Queen was already introducing her to others, and Magdalena found herself surrounded by young courtiers of both sexes.

She went into dinner with a splendidly attired young dandy who said his name was René. "And this is my sister, Hortense. *Ma foi*, how one is a fool to bring one's family into exile with one! How can one expect to find favour with a good-looking girl with a sister perpetually at one's elbow?" His eyes, which were the same sandy colour as his hair, were mocking, but Magdalena noticed they missed nothing of her appearance. Hortense, with the same coloured hair, but with dark brown eyes, laughed and said she would make Magdalena's acquaintance at a more propitious time. They went into the dining-room where a long table was set with ornate porcelain, crystal goblets and many candelabra.

★ ★ ★

Hortense was as good as her word, and on the following morning visited Magdalena in her rooms. They talked together for an hour or more; Magdalena discovering that the other girl had come from a château close to Paris which had been burnt to the ground and from which her parents had been forcibly removed to a prison where the last news she and René had had was that they were awaiting trial.

"For what, I ask?" Hortense said, her dark eyebrows raised. "For nothing — they led a blameless life. They were often at court, it is true, but if they liked dancing and masques that is no sin. We have not heard any news in months and I am afraid that René and I are orphans — penniless at that. Oh, Magdalena, where will it end? If you had seen sights such as René and I saw before we crossed into Flanders — *Mon Dieu*, it was terrible!" The girl shuddered and abruptly changed the subject. "Life here is tolerable — if you can stand children — and from time to time it is possible to forget what we have left. If you would like it I'll see you meet as many people as possible, and I'm sure René won't neglect you either."

This was certainly true, and Hortense was as good as her word. After three weeks Magdalena was able to report to Fourré that she was quite happy and had made friends with a small circle. Fourré was also serving as an extra curé to the Queen's household. "So we are both employed?" he said with a dry laugh.

"Very much so," Magdalena smiled, "but it is not all work, for tonight Hortense and René are taking me to a ball at the Palazzo Reale. It appears that an English man-of-war came into the harbour yesterday with despatches for the Chevalier Hamilton and the King is entertaining the captain and his officers."

"I am glad for you," Fourré said, his kindly face alight with warmth. "You've had enough of privations for a lifetime."

★ ★ ★

Magdalena dressed herself in the rose-coloured silk, and Bianca brushed her hair to fall into a single ringlet on one bared shoulder.

"Madonna," Bianca whispered, wide-eyed, "you'll be the loveliest lady at the ball."

"Thank you," Magdalena said, looking at herself in the mirror, "but one glance at my hands will ruin any chances I may have of attracting a beau."

"Bah, your hands are improving every day with the oil and lemon treatment I give them, and, anyway, M. René will think you're beautiful."

"Oh, M. René — " Magdalena dismissed him with a shrug — "he would flirt with any new face!"

"I think not, *signorina*. I've watched the gentleman and he can't take his eyes from you."

"Well, we'll see, won't we? I wish you were coming, Bianca."

"But that would not do at all!" Bianca was horrified.

"I don't see why not, you're just as pretty as any of the girls in the Queen's court, and with a little tuition you could soon learn the tricks of being a fine lady."

Bianca looked at Magdalena, her head on one side. "Anyone would imagine you have been listening to King Ferdinand; I think he believes all men are equal — a proper Jacobin, if you ask me!"

"Sh!" Magdalena cautioned. "It would not do for us to be caught laughing at the Queen's husband."

"Well, everyone else does," Bianca giggled, "and you'll have an opportunity to find out why tonight."

★ ★ ★

Hortense and Magdalena walked down the flight of marble stairs to the waiting carriage. Although it was now mid September and late evening it was still warm and the stars shone in a clear sky.

René talked during most of the drive about his prowess at fencing and dressage; his sister and Magdalena providing a counterpoint of 'ohs' and 'ahs' when the occasion seemed to warrant comment.

Magdalena was content to sit and let her mind become blank. Her young and ardent nature looked forward to the dancing and the opportunity of meeting new faces, but she could not forget for longer than a half an hour or so the dangerous situation in which her parents lived; it was not a prospect to encourage merry-making.

The Palazzo Reale was ablaze with candelabra, and the entrance into the courtyard was thronged with carriages and foot passengers. René told their coachman to stop, and they all three alighted and pushed their way to the door on the far side of the square. Here they were admitted by footmen and greeted by equerries who directed them to the stairs and the reception. Above the noise of voices and laughter Magdalena heard the strains of what must be a fairly large orchestra.

Slowly they followed the other guests into an antechamber where King Ferdinand greeted his guests. Magdalena saw at once why Bianca had ridiculed her monarch, for the King was gross and coarse featured, wearing clothes more suitable for a motley than to welcome a foreign power that brought aid. He was flanked by Sir John Acton, another gentleman who must be Sir William Hamilton, as Emma stood by his side, and a short, delicate-faced naval officer most correctly dressed. The King nodded to their salutations, wished them a pleasant evening and gestured them towards the ballroom.

It was at the moment that Magdalena entered and stood framed in the massive doorway that George Gates looked up from speaking with Josiah Nisbet and his other brother officers and fell in love.

13

GEORGE was not aware, of course, that this was the emotion which gripped him, for one is seldom conscious of the first occasion on which such an important and fatal impact is made. He knew only that he must lose no time in making the acquaintance of the beautiful girl who in some unspoken way stood out from the crowd about her.

It was not only her looks, which were startling enough, but an inward strength apparent in the carriage of her head and the calm way she acknowledged the conversation of her companions. Josiah Nisbet, Captain Nelson's stepson, followed George's gaze.

"Shall we ask to be introduced?" he drawled. "If not I'm going in search of another drink."

"You'd better not let your stepfather catch you over-indulging," a fellow midshipman grinned. "He'll have the hide off you and give you a lecture on *his* young days at sea where no one did anything but swab decks and catch polar bears!"

"That's grossly unfair," George growled. "The Captain's a better man than any of us are likely to be, and if you ask me he's too soft by half with our Josh here."

"Watch your step, Gates, or I'll start a mill with you right here under the nose of your haughty beauty."

George ignored the sally, and feeling he had stared long enough at the unknown girl moved away with a friend towards the supper-tables. It was while they were on their way to the chamber at the far end of the ballroom where long trestles were covered with snowy cloths and food such as they had only read about that an equerry stopped them.

"*Signori*, if I may interrupt a moment, I should be glad if you would allow me to introduce you to some of our emigré friends who are seeking a haven in Naples from your common enemy, the Army and Navy of the Convention."

George turned and found himself looking straight at Magdalena; he made polite murmurs and a perfunctory bow to

René and Hortense, hardly hearing their names, and found himself tongue-tied when the Italian courtier said, "And this, *signori*, is Mamselle la comtesse de la Bellefontaine." An aristo! In God's name he might have known that the lovely creature was totally out of reach of a farm-hand masquerading as a naval officer who, if the French had not declared war on England, would still have been acting as first mate on one of Mayman's vessels operating the North Sea trade.

Magdalena returned his self-conscious bow as he heard his brother officer break into stumbling, schoolroom French.

"*Signore*," the equerry said to George, "you do not know Italian or a little French?"

"None at all, I'm afraid."

"That is a shame indeed, but all is not lost, for a pretty girl who needs supper will certainly be able to make her needs known. May I show you to a table, here by a window overlooking the bay? Perhaps you can glimpse the lights from your ship."

George found himself with Magdalena's hand on his arm, and he could do nothing but escort her to the supper-room: a sight of René's face giving him sufficient encouragement to make a brave show of manners. Hortense seemed happy enough with George's friend, and the four of them sat down while a somewhat stilted conversation was carried on between the other girl and her escort. After a few moments Magdalena said to George, very slowly and in highly accented English, "You cannot speak my language?" George shook his head. "That is a great pity; my English is so bad, I regret I paid not enough attention in the schoolroom."

"I regret," George replied, "that I had no opportunity of learning French."

"Opportunity, what is that?"

"*Occasion*," the brother officer put in, apparently listening to two conversations at once.

"Ah, but that is terrible," Magdalena cried, looking at him, "and there is so much I want to ask you about your ship, about England, the war and what is going to happen to us all."

Food was now brought to them, and when the liveried servants had departed

George replied, "And there is so much I want to ask you." If he thought he was safe in the knowledge that she would not understand him he was mistaken, for she replied that there was little enough to know.

"I don't believe that," George countered.

Magdalena shrugged. George noticed she ate little or nothing of the rich fare placed in front of her, and discovered that he, also, had lost his appetite. "Do you dance, Monsieur?"

"Very badly," George stammered, having visions of the hilarity evoked in his fellow officers on the few occasions he had ventured to take part in any of the sets which they danced with the assurance of years of early training.

"Then I do not care to take part either, but I should, very much, like to walk on the terrace and try to pick out your ship." Magdalena was amazed at her own boldness, but she liked the strong, dark young man who had a dignity about him which reminded her of François and felt drawn to him in a way as none of the other men she had met in her short stay at Maria Carolina's court.

They walked on the terrace, hearing the noise from the narrow streets crowded about the palace, and leant on the balustrade where George tried to show her where *Agamemnon* lay at anchor. When she could not see it he put his arm about her shoulder and, holding her hand, pointed it in the direction of the ship.

She smelt of roses, lavender, mimosa, ambergris and the oils of countless other flowers, and the scent intoxicated George. Hardly knowing what he did he pulled her round to face him and kissed her on the mouth. Much to his surprise she did not slap his cheek or push him away, but said quietly, "I am glad you did that."

"Glad," he whispered, "how can that be?"

"You do not know what it has been like these past months, cut off from my family and feeling like a — like a — how do you say? — an outcast."

"Ah, but I do know," George replied, gaining courage from the warm comfort of her body so close to his.

"How so? Have you been a fugitive?"

George hesitated. In the three years

since he left Langetts he had spoken to no one about his past but, without knowing why, he trusted this stranger who had so suddenly come to mean a great deal to him. But if he told her, would she understand? How could she comprehend the despair aroused in him by his mother's faithless behaviour or the anger caused by the actions of the paid hand?

At last he held her a little closer and told her that he had, indeed, once had to run for his life and that he, like she, was cut off from his family and his home. "You and I have much in common it seems."

"Will you not tell me about it?"

"Yes, but not now, all I want to do is be near to you, touch you and be happy."

"You have been unhappy?"

"Very, but that is all over. One day, if we are fortunate enough to meet again, perhaps we shall understand each other's language sufficiently to make my story truthful."

"You are not going away?" Her voice was taut.

"We hope to stay two or three days; we have many sick on board and are short of provisions, but we came only to deliver despatches, and now that we've accomplished our mission we shall leave as soon as possible."

"But that is terrible! I had hoped you were here for a week — a month perhaps. It is too sad to find a friend and lose him in the same moment."

"You will call me friend, Magdalena?"

"Of course, you've made me happier than I have been since I left home; in fact, happier than I've ever been."

"Then I am glad." George led her to the far corner of the terrace, out of sight of the long windows of the ball-room and took her in his arms again, kissing her gently on her willing mouth.

How long they stood in mutual comfort of each other's embrace they could never be certain, but they were rudely shaken from their delight by the playing of the National Anthem.

Magdalena moved in George's arms. "We must go in. Shall I see you tomorrow?"

"I hope so, but if not tomorrow

on Sunday. I believe Captain Nelson is to return the hospitality of King Ferdinand and give a luncheon on board *Agamemnon*; he will expect all his officers to be present."

"Will you visit me if you are able?"

"With the best will in the world, but where?"

"Ah, I forget, we seem such old friends that I imagine you know everything about me."

"Everything and nothing perhaps."

Magdalena stopped walking and looked up at him. "Do you want to learn more?"

"I do."

"Then I am presently acting as a temporary lady-in-waiting to the Queen at her palace at Portici, which is five miles out of the city under the heights of Vesuvius."

"Are you not afraid of the volcano?"

"A little, but nature's horrors are more easily understood than man's cruelty to his fellow-men. If *you* are not afraid you can find a hired carriage just here, below the terrace, but, be warned, they ask shocking prices!"

"Then if I may, I'll wait upon you tomorrow if Captain Nelson permits."

Fate was kind in that Captain Nelson, who had been warmly welcomed at the Palazzo Sessa, the rented home of Sir William and Lady Hamilton, and was staying there as their guest, was invited to dine with Sir John Acton and saw no reason why some of his officers should not enjoy themselves as well, for no one knew, once they rejoined the Fleet, when they would land again.

★ ★ ★

Magdalena spent the intervening hours of the following day thinking of George.

The impression she had of him would have been unknown in Helmdon. The three years he had been away from the farm had altered him a great deal: although still well-built, his figure had fined down and he had lost the perpetual scowl which had spoilt his good features. He had learnt to hold himself well and had, unobtrusively, gone about the business of improving his speech and his manners.

Since Thomas Walker had taken him into his ship at the quay in Colchester he had worked hard at seamanship and had been promoted to first mate. His dreams of seeing the world had not been realised as Walker kept him with him, plying the North Sea trade. Only when war was declared against France had there been an opportunity to go further afield, and George had offered his services to Nelson and been accepted.

Thomas Walker had taken to the bottle on hearing the news, but after a three-day bout, coupled with threats, had failed to deter George from enlisting in the Navy, the old captain had resigned himself to his loss. His parting shots being double-barrelled in that he hoped if George was not killed he would not have the effrontery to present himself in Walker's cabin on the declaration of peace, expecting to slip back into his old berth. The sting of this sniping was somewhat eased by his presentation to George of his very handsome, gold repeater watch.

George's first days in *Agamemnon* were a disagreeable memory of unending work and painful scrutiny, but having long since learnt the lesson of saying as little as possible, his associates dropped their bantering and left him in peace.

Once the ship was commissioned and put to sea it was a very different story, for the fashionable gentlemen and those who had been, as Nelson, 'on the beach' for five years soon discovered that Gates was a skilled mariner. A guarded respect accompanied this unexpected disclosure, and more and more often was George called upon to give advice or demonstrate the handling of instruments, sails and lines.

By the time he came to Naples he was accepted as being no different from anyone else on board.

★ ★ ★

He went back on board *Agamemnon* on the long-boat with his mind full of Magdalena. He had, by now, encountered women in all walks of life but never until that evening had his heart and senses been touched. It was almost as if that part of his life which had been cut raw by his mother's behaviour had been healed in the warm softness of Magdalena's body. For the first time he knew that he wanted to bed a girl not only for the satisfaction of his own lust but for the gratification of some deep, almost spiritual need.

He made it his business to seek out his immediate superior as soon as he came aboard and ask for permission to leave the ship for some hours on the following afternoon. When this was granted he went to his cramped, shared cabin and slept dreamlessly.

★ ★ ★

It was late afternoon when he came to Portici Palace and he made himself understood with some difficulty. A footman showed him to an anteroom where he occupied his time examining (without really seeing) the pictures and objets d'art. He was bent over a collection of Roman coins when a gentle voice said: "George?"

"My dear," he stammered, his cravat suddenly too tight about his neck and his hands damp with sweat.

Magdalena was wearing the day-dress with a silk shawl about her shoulders. "Shall we walk in the gardens? There are so many children in the Queen's apartments that it is difficult to make oneself heard."

Her command of English had improved since the previous evening and she spoke a little less self-consciously and without too many pauses. She took George's hand and they went through several cool, darkened rooms until they found their way out into the hot sunlight in an enclosed formal garden. Here, in the far corner, was a gazebo of stone with delicately carved marble pillars; inside were benches in the same marble. Magdalena sat down and touched the seat beside her. George, still shocked by her beauty, which for most of the working day he had imagined was a romantic trick of his memory, followed her gesture. With a sense of wonderment he watched her turn towards him, her face uplifted to his. He kissed her, touching her cheek with his hand, and felt her arms go about him.

Once again they lost all sense of time, not noticing the setting of the sun or the fall of evening, until Magdalena disengaged herself and sat away from him. "I don't think I can bear you to go away from me."

"I feel the same way about you."

"What shall we do?"

"We can hope that we'll not be parted for long and we can write to each other."

"I was hoping you would say that. I've written a letter for you to take back to the ship." She pulled out a folded note from the pocket of her dress, and George put it in his dark blue jacket. "It will be good practice for my English, which M. Fourré always told me was my weakest subject."

"M. Fourré?" George questioned.

"Ah, he is my father's curé and my tutor." She began to tell him now of la Bellefontaine, her mother and father and Pierre. She talked little of the splendours of her home because, in truth, they had faded somewhat, and also because she sensed that this young man was unused to the style of life which had been her own. She spoke instead of her father's kindly attitude to his servants and tenants, remembering the Loire and the vineyards, the harvests and the other festivals. She told him, too, of François and his unenviable task of caring for his large family, but she could not bring herself to speak of the hardships of her journey; they were, anyway, diminished by her new-found joy in the company of another human being.

"Tell me about yourself," she pleaded.

And so, at last, he unburdened himself of the guilt that had been his constant bedfellow over the years, and she listened intently until most of the sordid tale was told.

"But you were right!" she cried. "Who but you could defend your mother's honour?"

"Do you really think so?" he asked.

"I do, and now you must forget the tragedy and think of yourself."

"I can't do that."

"Why not?"

"Because I can only think of you."

Magdalena hugged him. "That is the nicest thing I've ever had said to me, but I'm certain that when once you go back on board that horrible ship you will forget me."

"You don't mean that, do you?"

"No, for I shall never forget you."

There was silence, and they heard the soft whisper of the wind and the constant background music of the cicadas.

Suddenly George had to know if her emotions were as deeply involved as his own. "If," he said slowly, "we were to take more prize ships — Frenchies, I'm afraid — and I was to have my share of the monies, would you marry me?"

Her reply was calm. "Yes, I would."

And she knew as she made that promise that it was true, and she realised also that if Papa and Maman were to disapprove of her choice and would not recognise George as a fitting son-in-law she would give up her inheritance without a qualm.

It was very late when at last they returned to the palace. They made their farewells before coming into the wide entrance hall and walked hand-in-hand to the carriage which was waiting upon George's return.

"If you will not be coming to the luncheon on board tomorrow," George said in parting, "I'll do my best to come and see you before we sail." He stooped to kiss her forehead and saw tears in her eyes. "Don't cry, my love; if Fate was kind enough to bring us together it will not be so cruel to part us too quickly."

★ ★ ★

But in that he was wrong for Fate in the shape of a French man-of-war and three supporting vessels were sailing up the coast of Sardinia heading for Naples.

★ ★ ★

The following day, the Sunday of the King's reception on board *Agamemnon*, saw a swell of such magnitude in the bay that the visit was postponed until the following day. Provisioning of the ship was impossible and leave ashore cancelled. In the evening Nelson dined with the King and Emma and William Hamilton and was brought back to *Agamemnon* at first light on the following morning.

Here, with food and wine from the Hamilton's cellars, a breakfast was given for the English community while an elaborate meal was prepared in the galley for the King later in the day.

George was on watch, fretting at the waste of time spent in ceremonious matters when he might be going to Portici and worrying about the long sick-list which had been handed to him as duty officer. The midshipman who had brought him the information reported that hardly any stores had yet reached the ship, and fruit and water were in short supply.

"I'll see to it that as soon as His Majesty has disembarked we'll make a priority of victualling and fetching fresh water."

At noon, when George was thankfully relinquishing his watch a tender came out from the harbour. Lady Hamilton and all the other English guests crowded the rails to see a messenger being hoisted aboard. It soon appeared that he brought a note from Sir John Acton which stated news had been brought to the Queen of the presence of an enemy warship sailing in the direction of the Italian coast. From a hurried reading of the rest of the letter

Captain Nelson was left in no doubt that no Neapolitan ship was ready to put to sea and it was expected that he would honour his pledge of protection.

He could do nothing but obey, for he had, before he came aboard, seen twelve thousand soldiers (doubtless gathered from the slums of the city) ready to march towards Toulon in support of Hood's fleet and the loyal French citizens.

George was brought the news of imminent sailing by his servant whom he had despatched in search of a dish of tea. He went on deck to see his diminutive captain bundling his eminent visitors into the boats which had brought them to breakfast. Filled with despair at the prospect of not seeing Magdalena he watched as hands were piped to stations among the abandoned delicacies and rolling wine bottles and saw the sails fill out in the warm wind.

Until the last tip of Vesuvius vanished on the horizon he stood at the stern-rails and watched the piece of land where he imagined the palace at Portici lay.

14

WHEN Magdalena heard from another lady-in-waiting that Sir John Acton had sent despatches to Captain Nelson which had caused that gentleman to put to sea with spirited haste she had difficulty in restraining her tears. She was, at that moment, engaged in trying to persuade the Queen's five-year-old son to take a few mouthfuls of macaroni and it was all she could do to stop herself putting down the spoon and rushing to her own room.

As soon as she was free she sent for Fourré, and they walked together in the privy gardens where only a short time ago she and George had confessed their love.

"What is it, my child?" Fourré was aware that something momentous had happened to his charge, but he was totally unprepared for her sudden outburst of tears and heartrending sobs. "But, Magdalena, have you received some bad news?" Even as he spoke he thought this unlikely, for he had given strict instructions that any messages from la Bellefontaine should first be delivered to him.

"No, no, not what you think, *mon père*, but sad tidings all the same." She took out a small square of fine cambric and mopped her eyes and blew her nose. "You see, it's like this, I've fallen in love."

"Have you indeed?" This was an occurrence which he had long been anticipating. "But that is a cause for rejoicing not sorrow."

"It would be," Magdalena replied, regaining a measure of calm, "were it not that the man I love is an Englishman from the man-of-war which has been visiting Naples."

"An *Englishman*?" This was certainly more than Fourré had bargained for. "An Englishman — a good Catholic, I hope!"

"I haven't even asked him," Magdalena said in a voice tinged with exasperation; what had religion to do with finding comfort and an indescribable joy?

"Well, no doubt your Englishman will be returning to Naples, because now that the two countries have become allies it will be necessary for constant communication to be kept up between them. Our troops will march on Toulon, and with the fleet of the English at their backs will beat off the Army of the Convention and allow the royalists to keep control of the city."

Unfortunately this prophecy was to prove as false as the first Magdalena had heard in this selfsame garden.

By Christmas-time when Naples could be as bleak as any winter day in Britain, the Neapolitan army — or what remained of it — struggled back along the Aurelian Way to the capital. Lord Hood had been unable to hold the great port, and the republicans had recaptured half the French fleet and murdered those loyal to the ancient régime.

In Paris the broken Marie Antoinette was taken to the guillotine, her son disappeared, never to be heard of again, and her few, pitifully few, loyal retainers fled for their lives.

Maria Carolina, weak from the birth

of her latest child, was distraught and, finding nothing but gruff inarticulate sympathy from her boar-hunting husband, turned to the beautiful Emma for support. Emma brought her more than just friendship and a welcome distraction by singing and striking her famous attitudes, because the envoy's wife was acting as go-between for the court of the Two Sicilies and the English fleet. Captain Nelson had begun that correspondence with the Hamiltons that was to have such a momentous outcome on the lives of all three people concerned.

In the same fast frigate which brought despatches to the Queen came a letter to Magdalena from George. She was particularly unhappy at the time of its arrival as the great Christian festival had passed without a word smuggled out of France from her parents.

George's letter was brief, his handwriting bold and untidy, but Magdalena had worked daily at her English lessons with Fourré and she found the missive balm to the frustrated misery she suffered.

After telling her that their precipitous flight from the bay had been unnecessary as the French warship had vanished, he went on to say they had tried to put in to Leghorn for fresh water where they had discovered the enemy who refused to come out from neutral waters. In despair Nelson had returned to Toulon (at the time of the letter, not yet fallen in the republicans' hands) to give his crew the respite and provisions they needed.

"How long we shall stay here, I know not," George wrote, "but I wish, with all my heart, that the wind would bring us straight back to that bay where my love abides."

He ended with a sentence in passable French, adding, "My friend taught me this and tries to spare an hour or two to tutor me."

Magdalena's delight at receiving the news was tinged with anxiety at the fall of Toulon which was then only too well known at the Neapolitan court.

Emma Hamilton consoled her with the old adage that she would have heard the worst if it had happened and took a large bundle of letters for George, promising to give them to the next mail frigate which put in to the port.

Magdalena had other problems, for Naples was swamped yet again with a flood of French emigrés fleeing from a régime which now wallowed in a blood-lust that overstepped anything that had gone before.

As Magdalena's fears for her parents increased, her good looks and pleasant manners attracted a horde of emigré admirers to add to René's patent devotion. In vain Magdalena told them she was already pledged, and they merely scoffed at her vague remarks about a naval gentleman to whom she was promised.

"A naval officer!" René's comment was acid. "What does the heiress of the la Bellefontaine think she is doing allowing a fortune-hunter to give her the lie?"

Magdalena only smiled, not wishing to discuss George with the jealous young Frenchman. She had to admit that René and Hortense had become good friends, and she enjoyed dancing with the elegant scion of a noble family, but the emotion he aroused in her young breast was a slight stir on the waters compared with the tumult of her unexpected and whole-hearted love for an officer of the enemy's fleet.

Maria Carolina was in a constant state of anxiety about her nation. While she allowed Freemasons to carry on their secret meetings she had Sir John Acton set up a form of undercover police, and it was they who brought her the unwelcome tidings that the Jacobins were gaining support amongst the underfed rabble in the city. The Queen spoke to Ferdinand, and he took a couple of days from hunting and wandered among the *lazaroni* on the water-front returning to the palace with the news that his spouse should stop fretting as he could detect no unrest.

★ ★ ★

Spring came with warm breezes scented with blossoms from a hundred thousand flowers and bushes.

Magdalena was walking with three of the Queen's brood in the gardens of the Palazzo Reale when Bianca came to tell her that Fourré awaited her in the anteroom.

"Is something wrong?" Magdalena asked sharply.

There was a strange, hooded look about the maid's large eyes.

"*Non*, madonna, I think not, the padre merely asked me to bring you to him."

"Stay with the *fanciulli*."

Magdalena hurried upstairs and found Fourré standing at the window with his hands locked together behind him. He was not alone.

"Pierre!" Magdalena breathed.

"My lady." Pierre fell on his knees, taking her hand to kiss it.

"Tell me," she whispered, "my parents?"

"Are dead."

"Oh, no, oh no, not that."

Fourré came from the window, and in one of his rare gestures of physical contact put his arm about Magdalena's shoulder. "Sit down, my dear, I've ordered some wine and you must drink it while Pierre tells his story."

Somehow Magdalena found the chair and obediently took the wine-glass. Fourré motioned to Pierre to bring up a stool, and the three of them sat together in a corner of the ornate room.

Pierre began hesitantly: he had aged a great deal since Magdalena and Fourré had left for Naples nine months earlier, and his hair was white at the temples.

It appeared he had had little trouble in finding a passage to Gibraltar and thence to Bordeaux. "I will not trouble you with the details of my journey to la Bellefontaine, but I saw things that I was heartily glad you had been spared, milady, and more than once the republicans kept my papers for closer inspection, but eventually I came to my village and reported to the château. Here I was received with the utmost civility."

"My mother and father — they were alive then?"

"Oh, yes, I arrived about the beginning of November and all seemed pretty much as it had ever done; true, many of the servants had disappeared, but life went on in that part of the house which *le comte* and *la comtesse* had chosen as their own."

"What happened then?"

"One day in February, soon after daybreak of a cold and very windy day I was out in the fields exercising one of the two remaining horses when I heard gunshots and saw clouds of smoke billowing from the direction of the château. I turned the horse and went back, but as I approached the river, and was still hidden among the trees on the bank, I saw a large rabble of men and women surrounding the house. They were shouting, waving weapons in the air and throwing lighted, pitch-covered brands into the already-burning building. It was hopeless to do anything — I imagined that the shots had been fired by those still loyal to the house and nothing more could be done. After a morning of looting and plundering the store-houses they went away in the direction of Gien."

From a long way off Magdalena heard herself asking Pierre what he did next. She did not see Pierre glance at Fourré, who shook his head.

"When everything seemed safe I tethered the horse and crept up to the château which was practically burnt out and still smouldering. By a strange chance of fate, that part of the house where your parents were living had been least affected by the blaze, and it was here I found *le comte* and *la comtesse* lying close together shot through the head."

He could have added that the bodies were charred almost beyond recognition, but Fourré had warned him to be brief.

"So they died instantly?" the pale girl asked.

Pierre replied quietly. "Your father must have shot his wife and turned the gun on himself — they suffered very little."

Magdalena felt nothing but a desolation which was beyond tears. "Thank you for coming, Pierre. M. Fourré will see to your comfort, and now if you will forgive me I must go to my room."

Fourré and the groom watched in silence as she left them. "Thank God," the old priest said, "that we took her father's advice and brought her away in time."

"But she looked so terrible at hearing the news that I wonder if the shock will prove too great."

"I think not," Fourré said, "she is young and we have proved that her beauty harbours a great strength."

In her chamber Hortense awaited Magdalena. "Lie down and drink this," she said, "and I'll stay with you until you sleep."

Magdalena's last thought before the opiate brought her oblivion was not the unsupportable picture of her parents' death but a wish that George was with her to comfort her in her grief, while a small voice insisted that she was fortunate to have the continuing support of that good and selfless man, Fourré. And Pierre — the enigmatic one-time servant who had voluntarily chosen a rôle of unrecognised protection — what right had she to such devotion?

★ ★ ★

It was a terrible summer in Naples. The court was in mourning for Marie Antoinette, the weather was abominably hot, despatch frigates bringing news of fleet movements brought the unwelcome tidings that Nelson, while ashore with a party of men attacking the port of Calvi, was blinded in his right eye by a splinter of stone from an enemy shot.

To crown it all Vesuvius erupted with more force than it had done for two hundred and fifty years.

The city, stinking in the heat, forgot its political differences in a united prayer for salvation from the molten lava streaming down the sides of the volcano.

This supplication was heard and the city was saved from oblivion, but another menace appeared in the wake of averted disaster in the shape of disease. Thousands of unwashed bodies, hundreds of unchecked cows, pigs and starved dogs, together with the overpowering heat, contributed to the miasma that was omnipresent, and a virulent, bloody flux of the bowels tormented the inhabitants.

Sir William Hamilton, that most fastidious of men, fell foul of the diarrhoea and caused Emma a great deal of anxiety as he momentarily recovered only to fall ill almost at once.

But of more consequence to Magdalena was the fact that Fourré, who was more of a father-figure to her than before, was stricken with the illness. A harassed and exhausted physician wrote out a receipt of herbs and prescribed a light diet of rice and boiled water. Magdalena watched in growing despair as the priest grew weaker and weaker; she had excused herself from her duties as royal nurse-maid while she and Pierre kept up a constant vigil at the sufferer's bedside.

One day about a month after Fourré had first sickened he asked Magdalena to send for one of the palace chaplains. "And, my dear child, please open the wooden box on the table next to my altar."

When she obeyed Magdalena found a leather drawstring purse which she brought to Fourré. "Open it," he said, with his eyes closed and his swarthy face ashen against the pillows. "Those are the jewels which your mother gave to me in trust against the day of your marriage or my death. Now that the latter is fast approaching I know it would be her wish that you should receive them." His voice faltered, and Pierre raised his head to allow him to sip some water from an invalid's drinking-cup.

"Oh, *Mon Père*, you must not leave

us! The world cannot spare a good man like you, and Pierre and I will be lost without you."

"No you won't, you are young, my child, and have known and survived sufficient bereavements to give you strength to carry on alone. Besides, you will not be alone, for M. George will return to your side."

"I hope you are right, but I despair of seeing him again."

"Never despair, Magdalena, for the message of God to his children is to have hope."

A priest came in, and after taking Fourré's hand and kissing it Magdalena and Pierre went out of the room.

Fourré died during the long, still watches of the night when Pierre alone sat with him. He delayed breaking the news to Magdalena until the laying-out was over and the wasted body nailed into its coffin. It was Hortense who brought the sad tidings, and it was she and several of Magdalena's other friends who knelt with her in the palace chapel for the short service which preceded burial outside the city on a hilltop overlooking the bay.

Magdalena suffered more after Fourré's death than she had over the demise of her parents, whose very existence seemed to have acquired something of the fantastic in her mind. Was she really a countess, born to luxury and wealth? She began to brood and would sit motionless in the stone arbour of the little garden oblivious of her surroundings. It was after one of these bouts of accidie that Pierre suggested she should try and find François' brothers.

"I've tried, Pierre, and it's hopeless; all the palace officials can tell me is that the Baron boys came to court but left soon after to join the royalist army in Toulon."

"Well, would you like me to go to Castellane with letters for M. le duc?"

Magdalena shook her head. "Don't leave me, you are my sole link with the past, and if anything were to happen to you I think I'd lose my reason."

"Then may I suggest you buy a couple of horses and we could ride? You might join the King at hunting!"

"What! And watch him tear his victims to pieces? No, I'll not hunt, but the riding sounds a good idea."

It was to prove her salvation, for she found a growing dislike of her rôle in the Neapolitan court and yearned for the day which would bring George back into her life. The despatches which came to the Hamiltons and forged the bonds between them, Nelson and the Queen were borne in sloops and frigates which also carried letters between Magdalena and her lover. If George's were short and to the point, hers were lengthy and full of details of her life at Maria Carolina's beck and call.

One letter Magdalena received was a missive which was full of sympathy for her in the loss of her parents written from Leghorn. It told of futile efforts to engage an evasive enemy. "Captain Nelson is almost in despair at coming to grips with the slippery Frenchies."

* * *

The months, leaden-footed, crept by into years with Naples a hot-bed of rumours, fears and genuine alarms: Jacobin sympathisers were rounded up and sent to prison while Maria Carolina worked hard to keep friends with the English who seemed in 1796 to be Naples' only remaining ally.

Naples was in dire need of friends, for France, perhaps self-sickened of the increasing bloodshed of its own people, turned its attention to killing and conquering the citizens of other nations. Holland and Belgium fell, followed by the Savoy. By late spring the enemy was at the back door, and it was led by a brilliant young general called Napoleon Buonaparte.

Ferdinand, at severe odds with his wife and Acton, agreed to sign an armistice. Maria Carolina was in a state of collapse, and to cap it all the Lords of the Admiralty decided that the Mediterranean fleet should be recalled.

Magdalena heard the hateful news from Emma who carried a letter from George with her. Lady Hamilton was at her most voluble in declaiming the cowardly action of the King of the Two Sicilies which she was certain was the reason for the recall.

"How can they be so ungrateful, these

Neapolitans, after all we English have tried to do for them?"

"They are frightened," Magdalena said with resignation.

"Ferdinand is a coward! His wife makes two of him!" And she bustled off to her daily meeting with Maria Carolina.

George's letter was from England and had been relayed through several mail-frigates to reach her. It appeared that in June *Agamemnon* had been ordered home and Captain Nelson had volunteered to remain behind in another ship while an ailing commander took charge of his old ship. "It is not the same at all without Nelson," George wrote, "and if rumour is true and he is to come back here I shall ask to be transferred."

It was well on into the following year before Magdalena heard again from George, and he could only tell her that his hopes of being reunited with Nelson were bleak as his old Captain, now promoted Commodore and soon to be Rear Admiral, had been engaged in much active service, which kept him away from England. This brought him recognition and honours but did not satisfy George who wanted nothing more than to be taken on again by the clever little sailor and come with him into the Mediterranean. "Meanwhile all I do is hang about dockyards at Deptford watching my ship fitted out and longing for you."

Then, when Magdalena had almost given up hope with the rest of the court who were able, as she was not, to lose itself in gambling, drinking and furtive love-affairs, Acton received word that the English were returning in strength: they had seen enough of the martial aims of the New France to assert themselves again.

At almost the same time as these welcome tidings came to Acton, the Hamiltons heard that Nelson had had to have an arm amputated after a fight off the Spanish islands of the Canaries. Emma was unable to sing or cheer the Queen with posing with her shawl and Grecian urns.

Magdalena had no first-hand news until a hastily scrawled, jubilant letter from George told her that Sir Horatio

Nelson, now happily recovered from his severe wound, was to break his flag on *Vanguard* in the new year of 1798 and that he, George, was now transferred to assisting with the working up of the ship. He hoped to sail before too long.

This, although Magdalena was not to know it, he did on 29th March when Nelson took up his command and George was posted to one of the supporting frigates as first lieutenant.

In fair weather the English fleet put into Gibraltar and at once the questioning began: were the French in the Mediterranean or not? It was well known that if they were Nelson was going to find them and trounce them.

This proved more difficult than anyone had imagined, and to add to the difficulties foul weather sprang up and *Vanguard*, despite her admiral's seamanship, lost two masts. Nelson had to suffer the ignominy of being led by one of those under his command into safe anchorage off Sardinia. George's frigate lay near by.

Tantalisingly, by June *Vanguard* was sufficiently re-fitted to sail within sight of Ischia, an island in the arms of the bay of Naples. George sent letters ashore with those destined for greater personages than the love of his heart.

Magdalena could hardly believe her good fortune when Pierre brought her the sealed missives. He was happy to see her face alight with joy and with the patience that comes of thankful but hopeless love; he stood a little way off so that she could read in peace.

"Oh, Pierre," she called when she came to the end. "Is it not wonderful, M. George was within sight of Naples when he wrote the last of these. He prays that the English fleet will soon flush out the French and send them to the bottom of the sea so that he may come once again to see me."

★ ★ ★

But it was still not to be easy. Nelson had difficulty in finding safe places to water and provision until at last in Sicily he found willing vendors of livestock, chickens, fruit and vegetables.

This was the latest news Magdalena,

or anyone else in Naples, was to hear for a month, and it was now near the end of July.

The tension at the court built up to the extent that quarrels broke out daily, and the wining and gambling increased. Only the faithful, with Emma and Magdalena, took a little time off to pray.

And then at the beginning of September one of Nelson's frigates, the *Mutine*, came into the harbour bringing the news that the English fleet had finally found the French skulking in Aboukir bay and had won a resounding victory.

At once differences were forgotten. Captain Capel, who brought the momentous news, would have been fêted for days, but he pleaded he had to travel overland via Germany to bring the momentous news to England. "Our victory would have been perfect if only we had managed to finish the odious Napoleon at the same time; he was not too far off either, with his army, but there, we must he grateful for the daring and brilliance of Sir Horatio which led us to burn most of the wretched enemy fleet."

Magdalena, for the first time in those five dreary years, felt a glimmer of hope. A hope immediately dispelled by fear that George might have been a casualty of the fighting. She sought out and found Emma. An Emma transformed into a living tribute to her friend Horatio, for she wore earrings of little anchors, a shawl covered with the same small emblems and a sash which proclaimed her joy at the victory.

Before Magdalena could speak, Emma was going into raptures, "My dear countess, if you could see the Queen! She has never been so happy since her sister's death! She is wild with gratitude for what Nelson has achieved in the saving of her country."

At last Magdalena was able to ask about the number of men lost.

Emma hardly heard her. "Oh, I think we may have lost a man or two, but the carnage among the French was enormous." She kissed Magdalena. "Don't worry, your George will be quite safe."

Magdalena wished she felt the same complacent optimism; and found herself thinking it was a pity that Hortense and René had left Naples at the uncovering of the Jacobin movement in the city and sought refuge in a safer place in Germany. At least Hortense would have prayed with her and René partnered her in a dance to help pass the days of waiting.

And there were to be many of these before at last one of the few remaining seaworthy frigates of the Neapolitan navy came flying into the harbour to announce that within two, perhaps three, days, some of the victorious English ships would be putting into Naples.

Magdalena found herself on the edge of breakdown. All the perils, the hardships, the near-intolerable life at court, the overwhelming deaths of her parents, Mamselle and Fourré suddenly crushed her in the frustration which centred on *which* ships and *which* officers would come to Naples.

Pierre, so used to the moods of his mistress, saw the crisis and gently suggested rides into the hills. She consented to go, knowing that she would hear nothing for two days at least.

On the second day two ships were sighted, and many small boats put to sea, the King's and Sir William's among them, but it was not *Vanguard* they greeted but the vessels of Troubridge and Ball. They were given a tremendous reception, but it was Nelson that everyone was awaiting, and the two Englishmen brought the news that *Vanguard*, with a broken mast, was being towed by *Thalia* and would arrive within a day or two.

Magdalena, oblivious to the preparations at the Palazzo Reale and the Palazzo Sessa for royal receptions of the heroes, went to offer gratitude and prayer in the chapel. *Thalia* was George's ship.

15

ONLY a handful of people remained at the Palace Reale on Saturday, 22nd September, 1798. From early morning almost everyone prepared to put to sea or line the promenade — all were in a holiday mood, for was not the French fleet utterly destroyed? Was not the lurking enemy which only wanted to pounce stopped dead in its tracks?

Of the people who remained the Queen and Magdalena were two: the first because she preferred to greet her saviour within the state-rooms of her home and the second because she was too afraid of the news which might await her. Even if she had wished to accompany any of the gaily dressed parties who bobbed out over the waves, no one had seen fit to ask her; the King was accompanied by his own favourites, and Emma Hamilton forgot her young French friend in the excitement of seeing the conquering hero she had not set eyes on for five years.

Magdalena knew that the other English vessels which had preceded *Vanguard* were now lying in the yards of Castellmmare, and she expected that the damaged 74 gunner and her escort would be underway for the same naval base as soon as the greetings were over.

Bianca and Pierre went to join the throngs on the seafront. "Oh, madonna! You should have heard the bands, the cheering and the music. Why, even the opera house had its doors open, with the orchestra playing the English National Anthem. There were hundreds of boats in the bay, and birds were set free to show the joy of all the people. To think we've lived through all that nightmare!"

"Have we?" Magdalena thought. "If it's over what am I experiencing now?" But Bianca was rushing on with a description of how Sir Horatio had at last come ashore.

"The King was first, stepping out of his gold barge and shouting just like the rest of us, and then came the admiral with Sir William and Lady Hamilton. She looked like an angel, and

Sir William seemed brighter than for a long time, but oh, madonna, the poor little admiral!"

"What was the matter with him?" Magdalena enquired sharply.

"He had a bandage about his head and looked so frail and wan. I didn't know he'd been wounded, did you?"

"No, but in his despatches he never mentions himself."

Bianca looked at Magdalena contrite. "Oh, my lady, I've forgotten in all the excitement to ask if you have heard from the *signore*?"

"Not yet." Magdalena's voice was unemotional.

"But you will, you will. I've prayed to our Blessed Lady and to St. Januarius every morning and every night that he will be restored to you, and I know you'll not be disappointed."

★ ★ ★

In the afternoon Magdalena had a chance to see Nelson herself. She was sent word that the Queen, who had spent the morning in tears and laughter, was to receive Emma and the admiral, and Maria Carolina desired that as many of her children as possible would be on hand to pay their own homage.

Magdalena stood in the background while the Queen poured out her very genuine gratitude to the exhausted sailor.

"If it were not for you, all Italy would be under the thumb of that dastardly army of the French — how can we ever thank you?"

"Don't worry, your Majesty," Emma said, making the grandest of curtsies, "Sir William and I shall see Sir Horatio is afforded every comfort and honour."

After glasses of sparkling Asti had been handed around the party from the Palazza Sessa left. Emma caught sight of Magdalena as she stood firmly holding the hands of the youngest prince and princess by the door. "Oh, my dear countess," she whispered hurriedly, "I've had a quick glance through the list of casualties and I cannot see the name of Gates among them."

Magdalena felt a small stir of life in her heavy heart, and she gave the children to their nursemaids, telling them she would come to them later to read them a bedtime story.

She went to her own room, that room which had cost her nearly all the gold which she and Mamselle had secretly smuggled from la Bellefontaine, and fell on her knees before the crucifix on the wall away from the window. She had no idea of how long she had been there, when she heard a knock on the door. Half dazed she called "Come in" and turned to see Bianca in a state of suppressed excitement.

"Oh, madonna — what did I tell you?"

"No, Bianca, it cannot be true!"

"It *is* true, madonna, M. Gates is in the anteroom."

Magdalena, without waiting so much as a moment to glance in the mirror, ran out of her bedchamber and down the marble corridor to the drawing-room.

At the window, in almost the same attitude adopted by Fourré when he broke the news of her parents' death, stood George.

He turned as he heard her come in and, arms outstretched, enfolded her in his embrace. As he kissed her he found her cheeks wet with tears. "Oh, my love, it has been so long and so horrible. Let me look at you."

He led her to the open casement where the dying sun of one of Naples most magnificent sunsets turned her pale cheeks to a gentle, rosy glow. "You are even more beautiful than I remember."

"Oh, George, can it be true? Are you really here? Tell me I'm not dreaming."

"The days of dreaming are over, Magdalena." His tone was sombre, and Magdalena looked up at him swiftly. She saw in the dusk that he had aged much during their separation and there were lines about his mouth and eyes which had not been there before.

"You are well?" she asked. "Not wounded."

"No," he answered, "my body is untouched."

"What is it then?"

"I don't want to speak of it now nor spoil these moments of our reunion. I've dreamt about seeing you again so often that, like you, I need reassuring that you are not a phantom."

"You are tired. Where have you come from?"

"Just now from the docks at Castellmmare."

"But that is miles!"

"Yes, I hired a horse. I'd not be surprised if it has dropped dead for I rode it into the ground, poor nag!"

"I'll send Bianca to Pierre and he will look after it while you and I have some supper together."

"That would be most welcome as I've not eaten since breakfast."

Magdalena tugged the bell-rope and she asked the footman to send her maid to her. Bianca dropped a hurried salute to the pair of them and went off as she was asked to find food and Pierre.

"Who is Pierre?" George asked as he took her in his arms again.

"The groom who escaped with me."

"How did he come back? I thought he returned to your home."

"He did, but he returned four years ago with — but all that can wait until tomorrow."

George kissed her again with an intensity which Magdalena found almost frightening but which, at the same time, aroused the dormant passion which she had been at such pains to conceal for so long. "If I had my way I'd take you out of this great barracks of a place and into some healthy place where we could be alone together and at peace."

"That would be wonderful," Magdalena agreed, "somewhere in which to be together and order our own lives." She broke off as a servant came with a loaded tray. While he laid a spotless cloth on the small table, she and George stood at the window watching the sky turn from soft apricot to a luminous darkness.

Bianca reappeared. "Shall I wait on you, madonna?"

"No, thank you, Bianca. M. Gates and I have so much to talk about."

Bianca departed, shutting the door softly behind her.

"And I am on watch at midnight."

"Not at Castellmmare?"

"Yes, indeed at Castellmmare."

"But that is impossible."

"Impossible but true. My captain gave me leave to come to you only on the understanding that I returned at twelve."

"You have so short a time and there is so much to tell, so much to hear." She helped him to some cold fish with a highly seasoned sauce. "Tell me about your home — did you go to see your mother?"

George looked up at her. "Yes, with your memory to guide me I was brave enough to return to the farm."

"And what did you find?"

"That my mother was dead in childbirth."

"Oh, I'm so sorry."

"I was not," George said, levelly, "she never cared for me and she was bearing that devil's child."

"And the child?"

"Dead also, although my sisters — foolish women — cried at the memory of the poor little bastard's demise."

"What of the man?"

"Oh well, fortune smiled upon me there, for I'd not killed him as I'd feared; his head was broken but he recovered. When my mother died he tried to assume the tenancy of the farm, but during the time he was throwing

317

his ill-found weight about Samuel, my father's brother, came home. My twin brothers, Joseph and Reuben, were not yet old enough to have the running of the place, and my uncle found they were scurrying about like startled rabbits to the tune which Josh called. Samuel soon put a stop to that, he sold up his ship and came to live at Langetts; no longer young he knew he was no physical match for the man who had tried to take my father's place, and my inheritance, but he used more subtle means and soon had the girls and the twins on his side. After that it was a matter of waiting to see how long Josh could withstand the united onslaught. The final ousting came one evening when he was stupid enough to come home, drunk, from The Plough and tried to kiss my favourite sister, Lydia. She flew at him, and the twins picked up the fire-irons and chased him out of the doors. He hasn't been seen since."

"And now you'll leave the sea and return home?" Magdalena sat motionless in the candle-lit room, her food untouched on the gold-rimmed plates.

"No, I'll not do that. Uncle Samuel's trained the boys well and I'll not go back to it again, 'tis their inheritance now; besides, I've received some prize money over the years and I've no need to return, ever."

"But what will you do?"

"At the moment I'm not certain, but I have some ideas and when the time is ripe I'll tell you of them."

"How long are you going to be here?"

"Not long because I know Sir Horatio is anxious to be in England soon."

"But I cannot bear that you should leave me!"

"No," George replied. "Now, I've spoken more than enough, tell me all that has happened since last we met."

Magdalena began to cry, and in an instant he was kneeling by her chair cradling her in his arms, while she kissed the top of his head, put her face against his unpowdered hair and sobbed with all the pent-up emotion of the five long, dreary years he had been away.

For the first time she was able to speak of her parents and Fourré. George listened in grim silence until they heard the ornate clock on the mantelpiece chime ten.

"Oh My God." George groaned, "I'll have to leave you."

"Take Pierre with you for company, he can bring messages."

"But can you spare him?"

"For you, yes, and I'll not leave the palace until I have word from you."

"That will be as soon as possible, we've still so much to discuss."

"Yes, you've told me nothing of the battle that is the cause of the city's jubilation."

George muttered some comment which was inaudible to Magdalena, and kissing her, lovingly, on both cheeks bade her sleep well and keep herself safe until they were together again.

★ ★ ★

He did not come to see her until the following Wednesday, although she had received two letters from him. Much to her secret relief, Pierre seemed to have taken a liking to the foreigner and he

320

had made himself available for carrying missives.

"You look better, milady," he grunted as he brought her the latest letter, "and M. Gates seems to have recovered slightly."

"Has he spoken to you about the battle of Aboukir Bay?"

"No, he shys away from the subject."

Magdalena pondered this and was about to read what he had written when Bianca came to tell her that the Queen needed her urgently. With a sigh Magdalena put the note, unread, in the loose pocket of her dress.

Maria Carolina was full of the forthcoming plans for the ball Lady Hamilton was to give on the next Saturday. "It is Sir Horatio's fortieth birthday, and she is going to great trouble to make this an outstanding tribute to our best and dearest friend."

Magdalena wondered where this was leading until she gathered from the Queen's excitable chatter that it was her wish that Magdalena should go to the reception. "You have looked peaky of late, child, and dancing attendance on children can be very debilitating; I think it would do you good to have a little gaiety." She waved away Magdalena's gratitude and asked her to bring two of the children for their pre-supper visit.

It was dark when Magdalena returned to her room and was able to read George's letter. She was touched that he began it in very much better French than before, but found it soon lapsed into English as he told her that he would be coming early on the next day and asked her if she were able to take Pierre and meet him on the road to Castellmmare. "Perhaps we might find an inn where we can be away from the court and naval duties."

It seemed an age, but soon after dawn Magdalena was in the saddle of her roan mare riding down the coast to the shipyard. George, who had hired a hack, met them near a grove of olives where the road runs close under Vesuvius.

"There's a small hamlet not far back," he said after greeting them, "with a passable-looking *taverna*."

The place proved to be a one-storied whitewashed building with a vine-covered terrace overlooking the sea. Pierre went off to see to the horses, while George ordered coffee and newly baked bread.

"I'm so glad to see you," Magdalena told him.

"As glad as I you." It was a statement not a question, and when their breakfast was brought and they were alone again he went on, "I've thought a great deal about our futures while I've been confined in that pestilent dockyard and I've come to a momentous decision."

Magdalena regarded him, her heart beating faster than usual, "Tell me."

It seemed as if it were difficult for George to find the right words, but at last he said, "You're not really happy in Naples, are you?"

"No."

"And I never want to take part in another carnage like that in which we fought at the battle of the Nile."

"But I thought Aboukir Bay was a tremendous victory?"

"So it was, yet, have you ever thought of what victory really means? In cold hard facts it entails the slaughtering of one's fellow human beings — all of them someone's son or brother or husband — to what end?"

Magdalena was silent, glimpsing for the first time the reason for George's reticence about the event which had set Naples afire with admiration.

"Go on," she said.

"It was terrible, I saw sights I shall never forget, men with their clothes in flames hurling themselves into the sea which was already bogged down with corpses and the splintered remains of ships and rigging. Oh, Magdalena, I saw one powder-monkey, no older than my brothers when I first left home, running up the ladder with his cartridge in his arms, arrive on deck only to drop dead with the back-lash of the cannon he was feeding: and the stench of fire and blood still lingers in my nostrils."

Magdalena's eyes welled with tears. "But the enemy ships were burnt, and surely, thereby, all Europe is saved from further war?"

"Perhaps, but this new general, Buonaparte, or something, conquered Egypt with no trouble, and with the successes he has already had it is my belief a few fired ships will not stop him long."

"But Nelson won't allow him to recover his fleet."

"Nelson is a sailor, not a general."

"What have you in mind?"

George was silent while he drank some coffee and crumbled a roll of bread in his hand; sparrows, unnoticed, hopped under the table picking up the pieces.

"You are brave, Magdalena, and can suffer hardship. Would you come away with me if I can find a ship?"

"Of course, you do not have to ask, but what of your service in the navy?"

"Yes, that's tormented me night and day since the holocaust at Aboukir. If my friends believe I'm running from danger that's a verdict only to be expected. Yet I'm not afraid — only certain you and I can find a better life elsewhere."

"Where?"

"I don't know. I thought of the Americas, Canada perhaps. What I suggest, if you are willing, is to let Pierre wander round the ships in the harbour and see if he can discover a vessel outward bound: it's impossible to do it myself."

"You have only to ask," Magdalena said, "but when shall we go?"

"As soon as practical. Have you heard about this junket for Nelson's birthday?" Magdalena nodded. "I shall have a legitimate reason for being in the city that evening; if Pierre has any success, could you be ready to leave?"

"You know I can. What about money? My own stock is very low but I've my jewels which have lain unworn since they were given to me by M. Fourré."

"Keep them." George's tone was crisp, business-like. "I've enough to buy a passage." He looked at her. "You know you are everything and more than I remembered; half the women I've met would have had the vapours just listening to my plans."

"I want to be with you."

"Your inheritance?"

"Do you think there is anything left? Anyway, I should hate to return to my home. Bastien, my cousin, if he is still alive, can have the poor, burnt-out place. Shall I call Pierre?"

So they parted, arranging for Pierre to

find out what he could and carry letters between them.

On the ride back to Naples Magdalena broke the news of her possible departure and George's wish that Pierre should seek a merchant ship.

"Will you do this for me?" she asked.

"I would lay down my life for you."

"Let's hope that will not be necessary." Magdalena shuddered.

"May I ask one favour? Will you allow me to come with you as a servant?"

"You would do that for us? Leave everything behind you?"

"What have I to cherish except the trust put in me by Mamselle and M. Fourré?"

So it was on this understanding that Pierre, as soon as he had seen Magdalena safely back into the palace, set out through the bustling crowds for the port. He had nothing to report by evening but returned again after dark on his quest.

And it was while he sat drinking in a water-side *taverna* that he heard of an East Indiaman which had docked during his absence. Casually he threw some *soldi* on the counter and set out for the dock.

Here he found a trim ship about the same size as a frigate and asked to be taken to the master.

The man was English, stout and immensely strong. Pierre spoke but a few words of his language but managed to convey he wanted passage accommodation for three people. The master called in his first mate, and by gestures and demonstration it finally transpired that the ship was leaving on Saturday evening with a cargo of silks and Capodimonte china and did have room for three paying passengers. As security that he was in earnest, Pierre paid over the golden guineas which George had given him and indicated he required a receipt.

The sight of the English money appeared to reassure the master who had carried many of his countrymen home after they had made their grand tours of Europe. Pierre left him, sorry that his mistress would have to wait until morning to hear of his success.

Magdalena's first question upon hearing that she and George were to have an opportunity of making new lives for themselves was, "Where are we going?"

Pierre had to admit he had been unable to discover.

★ ★ ★

In the two days left to them, Magdalena, George and Pierre made moves to collect together as much as possible of their few possessions. Pierre hired a cart, and in the darkness of Thursday night transferred George's sea-chest from his lodging at Castellmmare to the ship in Naples harbour.

Bianca had to be told of her mistress's plans, and not to Magdalena's complete surprise broke down and cried. "You've come to mean to much to me, madonna, that I shall be lost without you. How can I serve another lady or return to the squalor of my home? Take me with you, please!"

"But we've no idea of our destination; it could be anywhere in the world and the conditions we'll face might be as bad as anything in Naples. Yet, if you really want to come I'll write to M. George."

So it was arranged that the four of

them would meet on the quay at ten-thirty on the evening of Nelson's birthday party.

Magdalena dressed with trembling fingers in a sea-green robe of silk and wore for the first time a necklace of emeralds and rose diamonds, the bracelet to match and several old and valuable rings. Bianca's expressive face told her that she looked her best.

"A highly unsuitable costume for boarding a ship," was Magdalena's comment.

"But don't forget I'll be with other maids and will have your winter cloak and a head shawl. Are you not a little frightened, madonna?"

"Not really, I'm sorry to leave Maria Carolina without a proper farewell, for she has been kind to me in her way."

"You have repaid that kindness a thousand times, and I'll remember to give the footman your note to deliver tomorrow morning."

The streets were more crowded than usual, and Magdalena threw a few *soldi* to the children who ran beside their carriage. Usually patient she could hardly wait to arrive at the Palazza Sessa for the ball which was to follow the dinner to which George but not she had been invited.

When Bianca had taken her cloak she went to the canopied ballroom where she was given favours of buttons and ribbons inscribed with Nelson's name. At a loss to know what to do with them, she put them in her reticule while her eyes sought out George.

She saw him at last, near a column fashioned after a Roman triumphal statue, talking with a group of officers. Almost at the same moment he saw her and, bowing, left them to join her. His clasp of her hand was reassuring. "Only an hour and we can slip away. Have you eaten?" When she shook her head he led her to the supper-room and found a footman who brought meats and glasses of champagne.

"Are you not eating?" she asked.

"No, after that banquet I doubt if I'll eat tomorrow either. Sir William's hospitality was lavish, to say the least, and we were served on new porcelain especially made in a local factory of which every piece had Nelson's initials and 'Glorious First of August' around the rim. Well, I suppose it helps those who were present at Aboukir to forget a little, although the admiral looked very queasy."

George forbore to mention the weather which had suddenly turned overcast with the wind whipping up the inevitable swell in the bay: he was afraid that the master of the merchant vessel would delay sailing, but prayed their whereabouts would not be discovered until they had put to sea. It would, in any case, be late on the morrow before either of them would be missed.

With some difficulty they forced themselves to join a set for two or three dances, and then Magdalena made an excuse of a sudden headache. George escorted her to her carriage and the waiting Bianca and returned to the ballroom.

It was raining now and the streets were empty and they arrived quickly enough at the Palazza Reale. Pierre emerged from the shadows as the vehicle came to a stop and said, loudly, that he would be glad if his mistress would look at her mare which seemed to be ailing.

In the confusion of the carriage returning uphill to the Hamilton's residence, the three walked boldly back towards the harbour. Magdalena hugged her cloak about her and was relieved when Pierre announced they had arrived.

The hand on watch allowed them aboard and led them to the master who eyed them with open curiosity. He, nevertheless, was polite and hospitable and showed them to two very small cabins, quite close to his own. He appeared to be surprised at Bianca's appearance, but Magdalena decided to wait for George to explain that she, also, was a passenger. In the meantime she sent her to bed.

In the cabin which was painted white, with a small porthole and two berths, one on top of the other, Magdalena slipped off her jewels and put them away. From the bag which Bianca had packed she found a nightgown and robe.

For the first time the full realisation of what she was doing struck her. This was the turning-point of her life. She and

George would now be living as man and wife. In the excitement of all that meant she could not help a restrained smile at the preparations which would have led up to her marriage from la Bellefontaine.

How different was this constricted cabin from the luxurious chamber which might have been hers! How different the nuptials from a complete absence of ceremony. Yet she knew that whatever happened between George and herself on this night would be more binding than any mass or marriage settlement.

After what seemed a long time she heard Pierre greeting George and listened with great relief as the latter talked with the master. Although she could not understand completely all they said she gathered from the tone of the conversation that all was well.

Ten minutes later George came into the cabin, the oil-lamp swinging in its gimbal with the motion of the sea felt even within the harbour; she saw his face light up with joy and relief as he saw her waiting for him in the lower berth.

"Thank God," he said, "we are leaving at dawn. The ship is stout enough and the master says he is used to heavier seas than any he is likely to encounter in the Mediterranean."

He came over and kissed her on the brow, lightly, while he undid his stock and then pulled off his highly polished boots.

Magdalena watched him, touched with love for the broadness of his back and chest, the slimness of his waist and thighs.

"Where are we going?" she asked as he climbed into the bunk beside her and took her in his arms.

"The Cape of Good Hope," he replied, "which I'm sure is an omen for our future together."

Other titles in the
Ulverscroft Large Print Series:

TO FIGHT THE WILD
Rod Ansell and Rachel Percy

Lost in uncharted Australian bush, Rod Ansell survived by hunting and trapping wild animals, improvising shelter and using all the bushman's skills he knew.

COROMANDEL
Pat Barr

India in the 1830s is a hot, uncomfortable place, where the East India Company still rules. Amelia and her new husband find themselves caught up in the animosities which seethe between the old order and the new.

THE SMALL PARTY
Lillian Beckwith

A frightening journey to safety begins for Ruth and her small party as their island is caught up in the dangers of armed insurrection.

THE WILDERNESS WALK
Sheila Bishop

Stifling unpleasant memories of a misbegotten romance in Cleave with Lord Francis Aubrey, Lavinia goes on holiday there with her sister. The two women are thrust into a romantic intrigue involving none other than Lord Francis.

THE RELUCTANT GUEST
Rosalind Brett

Ann Calvert went to spend a month on a South African farm with Theo Borland and his sister. They both proved to be different from her first idea of them, and there was Storr Peterson — the most disturbing man she had ever met.

ONE ENCHANTED SUMMER
Anne Tedlock Brooks

A tale of mystery and romance and a girl who found both during one enchanted summer.

CLOUD OVER MALVERTON
Nancy Buckingham

Dulcie soon realises that something is seriously wrong at Malverton, and when violence strikes she is horrified to find herself under suspicion of murder.

AFTER THOUGHTS
Max Bygraves

The Cockney entertainer tells stories of his East End childhood, of his RAF days, and his post-war showbusiness successes and friendships with fellow comedians.

MOONLIGHT
AND MARCH ROSES
D. Y. Cameron

Lynn's search to trace a missing girl takes her to Spain, where she meets Clive Hendon. While untangling the situation, she untangles her emotions and decides on her own future.